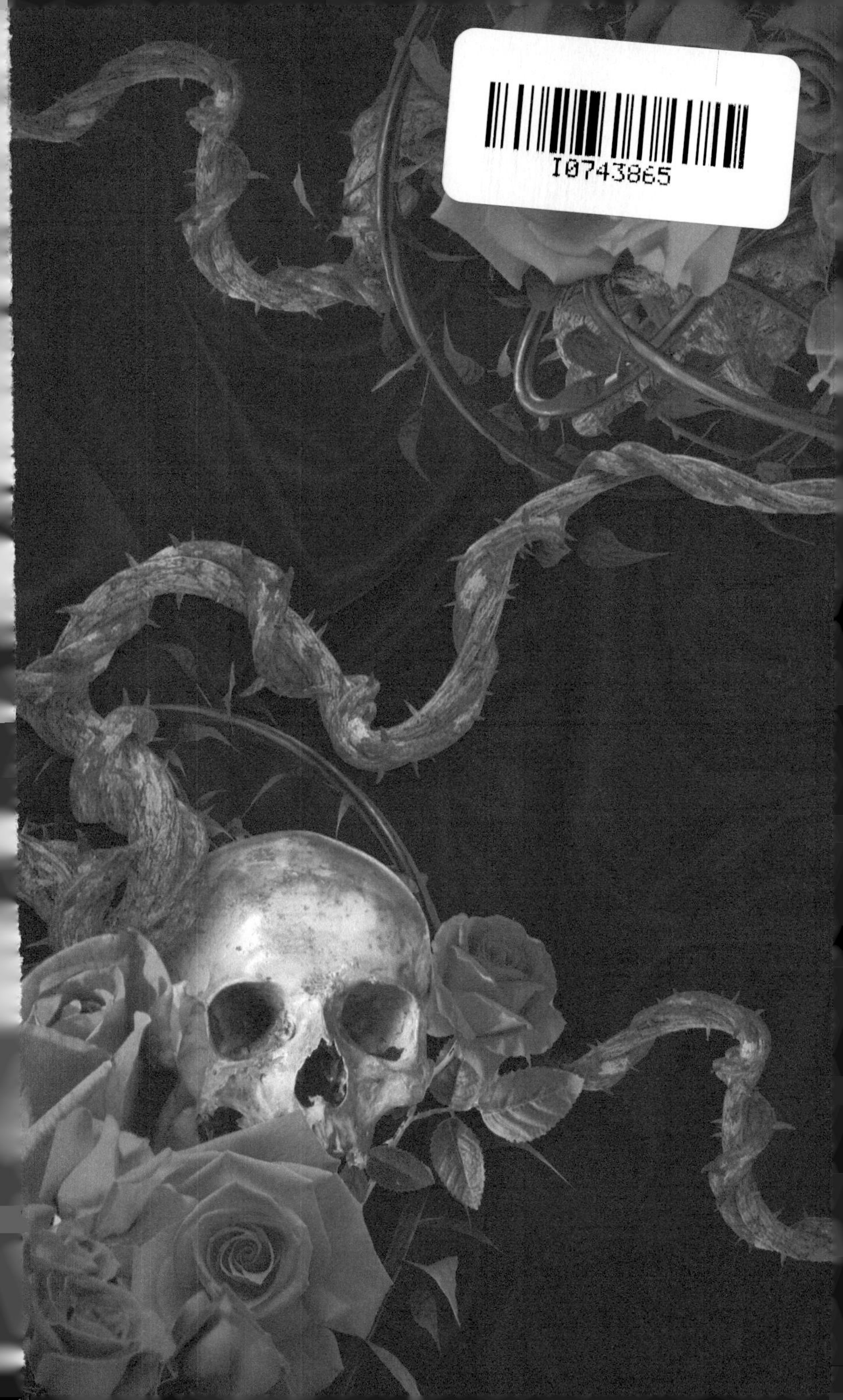
I0743865

STOLEN PARADISE

KINGS OF EDEN
BOOK TWO

MILA YOUNG

HARPER A. BROOKS

DEDICATION

To everyone who has found themselves in books

To all our readers for your incredible support

And to those of us who love cliffhangers...
(see what we did there LOL)

Love you all
Mila and Harper

CONTENTS

These monsters rule the city... and I've become their newest obsession.

I've been caught in a war between the three most powerful gangs in the city... and I'm trapped with the most dangerous of them all.

The Kings.

With each passing day, they lurk closer, their darkness pulling me a bit deeper. They push me, demanding everything I have when my world is falling apart.

Chaos is about to break out, and I'm finding myself craving the men who could just as easily break me. Ruin me. Kill me.

I vow to escape, but I'm losing myself to this world of lust and war.

The Kings of Eden don't have hearts. So they want mine...

CHAPTER ONE

EVE

As the man with fire blazing in his gaze stands before us, his words jab into my brain.

Me, this fire-horse riding monster's *daughter*?

No fucking way.

But then, why is Knox staring at me with such confusion and horror in his eyes? There's anger in there, too, like he's pissed he now has to choose between protecting me or killing me.

Knox had called the fire-breather Aris, too—is this the Aris he thought was possessing me? The one he was so desperate to kill when we first met? Has to be.

And if Knox is Death, a horseman, then that means Aris is also.

The danger level of this entire scenario just hit an all-time high. I am in deep shit.

Suddenly there's an explosion and glass flies everywhere. I shield my face as more gunfire erupts from seemingly everywhere.

Shit!

"Oh! This is where the party is!" Cassius's cackle has my head snapping up. I see him holding one of the Spades from behind and snaps his neck with ease. Before the man even drops dead on the floor, he's onto the next, punching him hard in the chest. The man's rib cage collapses and I wince at the loud crack.

A fierce roar has my attention swinging across the room to where a bear the size of a minivan is bulldozing through the masses, chomping down on anyone who dares get too close and tearing them to shreds.

A bear? Where the fuck did that come from?

The monstrous creature throws its head back, blood from its latest victim spraying everywhere, and when I catch a glimpse of its familiar yellow eyes, my stomach somersaults.

Dracon?

But how? I thought he was a dragon shifter. I've seen him shift before my eyes. How could he be a bear too? Can he shift into multiple creatures? I've never heard of a supernatural who could do such a thing.

These Kings are more powerful than I thought. Hopefully that's to our advantage.

Kat's scream tears through me and reminds me what I'm really here for.

Her.

Let the guys duke it out. I needed to get her out of this hell and to safety.

Frantically, I search the area for something to break the cage's lock, but find nothing but dead bodies. I crawl over to the closest one, which is laying face down in a pool of its own blood, and ignore the roiling of acid in my gut as I pat it down for it gun. Behind me, the sounds of carnage intensify and that alone makes me hurry. I find the dead guard's pistol tucked into the waistband of his pants—the poor fucker didn't even get a chance to draw the thing in the fight—and I seize it and jump to my feet.

My hands tremble around the thing, but I point it at the cage's lock with my finger on the trigger. "Get away from the door," I bark at Kat, who quickly shuffles out of harm's way. I've never used a gun before but there's no time like the present.

I fire two rounds, the weapon jerking my arms back from the force. Of course the bullets miss and ricochet off the wall.

"Shit!" I hiss and aim again. Trying to settle my shaky grip, I step closer and fire off another two shots. There's a clank of hitting metal, a spark, and the cage's lock swings free.

I rush over, yank it off, and toss it aside. The second I open the door, Kat rushes me, wrapping me in a hug. Her sobs of relief stab at my heart, and I hate that I was the one to put her into this situation in the first place. Even if it wasn't intentional.

"It's okay," I say to her as I pant. "You're okay."

She pulls back and nods, unable to find her voice.

"I'm going to get you out of here," I go on and drag her to her feet.

"Come on," I whisper harshly and help move Kat closer to the shelving units. Her legs wobble and she stumbles a bit, but I'm able to get us to it in one piece. Kicking milk crates aside, I press the gun into her hand.

She stares at it in horror. "You're going to need to climb up on your own. There's a window at the top. If anyone tries anything, shoot first."

She nods again, and it kills me to see her so shaken and weak. Especially knowing what a powerhouse of a woman she is. The Black Spades must've really fucked her up, and my heart clenches with guilt.

"I'll be right behind you. Now go."

That's all she needs because she grabs onto the shelving unit and starts to heave herself up toward the window I'd climbed in through.

I'm about to follow, as promised, but something makes me turn around, back to the fighting and where the Kings of Eden are locked in battle. The warehouse floor is covered in the dead, and from the looks of it, the smarter of the humans are now running for the exits. Franco is one of them—I spot him slipping out a back door.

Fucking coward.

Knox is covered in blood. It soaks his hair and runs down his face like some kind of macabre warpaint. His eyes shine with excitement as he looks over the death and destruction. At the same time, Cassius comes up to his side and runs a shaky hand through his blond hair. He's blurring again, his form vibrating like the night of the auction, when his demon was on the verge of taking over. Reaching into his pocket, he pulls out the little tin of powdered cocaine, opens it, takes a quick bump. A quick rub of his nose, then his teeth, and his jerky body seems to calm. At least a little.

The bear rears up on its hind legs and roars again,

but this time, its fur begins to recede and the muscles under his skin bunch and shift. Its giant form shrinks before my eyes, bones breaking and realigning, until a man stands in its place. A naked, hunk of a man.

Dracon.

A sheen of sweat coats his skin and he's breathing heavy, blood smeared across his mouth. In any other situation, I may've ogled them and how terrifyingly gorgeous they looked, each with murder in their eyes, but with them all now facing down Aris, a fucking horseman of the apocalypse, but now wasn't the time.

"Wait a fucking minute." With a barking laugh, Cassius hooks a thumb the fiery horseman's way. He seems unimpressed. "*This* is Aris?"

Aris's head cocks his way, and his lip curls up in obvious disgust. "You dare utter a sound to me, creature of the underworld?"

"That's a roundabout way of saying demon," Cassius replies, annoyance clear in his tone. "And yes. Yes I do."

I know a lot of supernatural types—I've met some odd ones while working at Kat's Kradle—but he's the first demon I've met. I didn't think they were real for a long time. It definitely isn't what I would've guessed for Cassius when I first met him, but now that I know demons are real, it makes a shit ton of sense.

I hold my breath, well aware of the danger looming so close to the surface. The air is thick with the budding tension.

"Filth," Aris spits. "Crawl back into the pits where you came from."

Cassius laughs again, but this time, it's a manic

sound. "I would, but they don't want me, either. Got kicked out for bad behavior."

His gaze swings to Dracon. "Are we killing this bastard, Drac?" he asks and bounces on his toes. "I'm getting bored."

Aris grins. "You can try."

Gritting his teeth, Dracon gives him the subtlest of nods, but that's all the other two need to surge into action. Knox releases a battle cry and charges. As he whirls the deadly Mortem Blade, Aris extracts a long flaming sword and blocks his attack easily. Knox steps forward and swings again, but even though he moves smoothly and lightning fast, Aris always meets his blows. It isn't long before his vicious roars turn into bellows of anger and frustration.

Aris only laughs.

Cassius jumps in to help Knox, trying to swoop in from the side, but Aris is able to dodge his blows, ducking and weaving at the same time he meets Knox's attacks. It's an incredible and terrifying thing to behold —so much grace and power in a single being. I always thought the Kings were the most feared and deadly creatures in existence. Yet, Aris is taking on two of them without breaking a sweat.

Cassius is fighting with fists, knees, and legs, but he still can't seem to land a single blow. Every time the Mortem Blade hits Aris's fire sword, blue sparks and red flames explode from the weapons.

When Dracon sees an opening, he lunges, jaw extending as he partially shifts again. This time to an animal with black fur and a long, protruding jaw and sharp teeth. A wolf, it seems, because when he slashes his hands Aris's way, they're transformed into razor-sharp claws.

Four deep gashes appear in the metal of Aris's armor, but the godlike man is too fast for anyone to spill his blood. Aris nails Dracon across the temple with the blunt end of his sword, hard enough to splinter bone. My heart skips a beat as Dracon is thrown off his feet. His eyes widen in shock, like he can't believe someone actually got the upper hand. But it's only seconds before he's trudging back into the fight, his powerful jaws snapping around Aris's leg, crunching the armor's plates.

Fire blazes across Aris's and Knox's crossed blades. I can see sweat clinging to Cassius's forehead as he pummels his fists into Aris's side, but either he's too focused on Knox and the Mortem Blade, or Dracon's and Cassius's attacks are nothing to him because he doesn't flinch from either. I know both men are stronger than any man or supernatural I've ever seen.

I don't know what it is, but just watching these powerful men try to destroy each other has the chaotic magic inside me humming to life. The air around me begins to buzz and rush past my ears, and the same dread I always feel when my power surges grips me like a vice.

Oh no. No, no, no, no! Not now!

Energy whips through me, amplifying quickly and sending me stumbling backward. The walls of the warehouse groan, seeming to bow in as if pulled inward by a magnet. Or black hole.

Sensing the change first, Knox's head whips my way, dark hair plastered to his face and gaze wild.

Aris takes that moment to unleash an inferno of magic and fire. It sears my skin, and a scream tears from my throat. The intensity of the heat burns my lungs, making breathing near impossible.

A series of thunderous booms come next, each one punching me through the chest.

"Yeeesss!" Aris bellows with glee. "The power! Can't you *feel* it?"

When the fire dies away, I peek out and see Cassius and Dracon have been thrown across the warehouse—Dracon into another shelving unit that's collapsed on top of him and Cassius facedown feet away from me, his arm twisted at an odd angle.

My pulse races through my veins.

Are they...*okay*? I never thought that the three of them could actually die. Now that seems like a very real possibility.

Knox is the only one standing, but even he's been pushed back from the blast, arms shielding his face from the blaze.

Aris whirls on me with a pleased smile, his eyes flashing an unnatural red, and I freeze on the spot.

"My offspring. My perfect little destroyer," he says.

An ominous chill radiates down my spine and another wave of power radiates from me at his words. The walls around us whine and groan as the wind picks up, tossing up my hair and whistling through the rafters above.

"What have you done!" Knox shouts as he charges

Aris again, Mortem Blade cutting through the air. When Aris blocks his attack again, Knox spins, lashing out, but they move toe to toe, matching each other's movements like some fucked choreographed dance. Each cross of their weapons enrages Knox more and more.

"You've ruined the natural balance!" he gasps between strikes. "The universe will collapse!"

They lock swords again, but Aris stiffens his elbows, pushing the two deadly weapons closer to Knox's face.

"You say that like it's a bad thing," he purrs.

Shoving the deranged horseman back, Knox manages to free himself, and more blue sparks erupt between them. There's murder in his eyes. Murder, hatred, and disbelief.

"Eve." A harsh whisper comes from my right, and when I glance down, I see Cassius lifting his head to peek up at me. He's rolling out his shoulder, his arm readjusting and popping back into place on its own. *Freaky.*

"Listen to me," he says quickly and grimaces in pain. "We need to banish this mother fucker. He's too strong. And I may know how to do it, but I'll need your help."

My help? What can I do? Especially with my magic so out of control.

Crouching low, I shuffle closer to him.

Cassius is struggling to get up, but with great difficulty, he manages to push himself up to his knees. His body is doing that strange blur thing, where he vibrates around the edges, and his eyes darken a shade as the demon pushes to the surface, even with the drugs in his system. In one swift move, he tugs off his shirt and tears it into two pieces.

"First, we need to draw a circle around the bastard in blood." He hands me the fabric and gestures to the dead Black Spades around us. "Soak this and use it. I'll take the other side."

I hold the torn shirt for a moment, wondering if I'd heard him right. But when he shoves his piece into a nearby bloody puddle and then whirls on me, eyes wide with urgency, I rush across the room to one of the sewer drains where a lot of the blood has flowed. Hot bile climbs up my throat as I soak the shirt in it, but I work quickly.

Cassius is already limping around the warehouse, dragging his shirt along the ground, painting the cement red, all while chanting words in an unknown language. Around me, my magic kicks up, causing the wind to whip by and the windows to rattle in their panes.

"Hurry!" Cassius shouts against the rising noise and chaos.

Following his lead, I use the bloody cloth to draw the other half of the circle around Aris and Knox as they continue to fight to the death. I rush to meet Cassius on the other side, and the second the bloody lines meet, black flames chase each other around the ring.

I leap back. I've never seen anything like it.

"Hellfire," Cassius says, the flames reflecting in his eyes. A sickly grin splits his face.

"What about Knox?" I ask him. If this is supposed to

banish Aris—to Hell or wherever—then wouldn't it kick Knox's ass too, if he's inside the circle?

"Hopefully he's smart enough to jump out at the last minute."

That doesn't help my anxiety any.

Cassius lifts his hands, palms facing out, and his body shimmers more. His demon dances across his face, contorting his features and making him look absolutely terrifying. All I can do is stand back and watch as he begins to chant again.

Behind us, Dracon is slowly pulling himself from the rubble. Now back in his human form, there's a deep gash across his forehead and a gnarly looking wound on his shoulder, and he's covered in dust and blood. His yellow eyes flick between us and Knox and Aris, as if he's trying to make out what Cassius is up to.

Suddenly, the fire rises, creating a barrier wall. I can barely see what's happening inside the circle. Not to mention that with all the commotion around us, I can't even hear the clang of metal on metal or the sounds of fighting anymore.

My worry spikes for Knox, and I'm not sure why. But thinking that he may be trapped with this madman in some alternative universe or sent to some other realm has my breathing and my magic speeding up.

He needs to get out of there!

"Eve, stop whatever you're doing!" Dracon yells against the tornado of wind and magic.

"I can't!" I bellow back. I already would've if I could. "I can't control it!"

"Yes. you can!"

Working against the unruly wind gusts, Cassius continues his spell. Pieces of wood and debris are being tossed about, and I have to shield my face from being hit with something or knocked out. Tall black flames lick the air, and the atmosphere seems to buckle in one last time before bursting outward in a massive explosion. Every window in the warehouse shatters and glass rains down on us from above.

All at once, everything stops. The wind. The dark magic. Cassius's chanting. The heavy pressure. Even the circle of fire has snuffed out, leaving only a ring of ash on the cement floor.

In the middle is Aris, laying on his back with his eyes closed, not moving. But I don't think we are lucky enough for him to be dead.

Wasn't Cassius's spell supposed to banish him? That had been what he'd said it'd do, right? So then, why is he still here?

And where the fuck is Knox?

After scanning the warehouse and seeing no sign of him, I try to step forward but Dracon's suddenly beside me, his unyielding grip on my upper arm.

"Don't move," he commands. "It may not be over yet."

"I don't get it," Cassius pants next to me. When his head whips to Dracon, there's desperation in his eyes. "He's not supposed to be here anymore. That spell should've sent his ass straight to Hell."

"This isn't a normal soul we're working with here," he offers as an explanation.

"I know, but I've seen it work on the most powerful of demons. Fuck, it even worked on Lucifer himself."

"Aris must be stronger than Lucifer."

Well, isn't that a fucking scary thought.

"Where's Knox?" I croak out, my voice sounding as frail as I feel. Every inch of me is shaking, and whether it's from the adrenaline, whatever terrible magic I have spinning inside me, or shock, I don't know.

Dracon's hand doesn't leave my arm, and I'm actually grateful. I may fall right over if he lets me go.

"Maybe he went ghost again?" Cassius suggests.

Went ghost? What does that mean?

"Maybe you sent him to Hell instead of Aris," Dracon replies.

"Fuck, maybe you're right." Cassius runs a hand over his face in a failed attempt to shake off his demon. His figure only seems to vibrate more, and he pulls out his tin of cocaine and takes a bigger hit this time, rubbing more across his gums afterward. Throwing his head back, I watch as the demon begins to recede. "Knox is going to kill me."

My knees finally give out, and now Cassius is holding me upright, too. My vision is blurring more and more by the second.

"I think we need to get out of here," Cassius says, "for her sake."

I don't hear Dracon's answer, but he must agree because I can feel myself moving, floating, but walking.

Then, I lose myself to the darkness completely.

CHAPTER TWO

DRACON

Watching Eve pass out has my heart aching more than any of the cuts or bruises I've gotten today. Luckily, I am there to catch her as she goes down, but when I pull her into my arms, I realize her face looks deathly pale and her head rolls to the side.

I don't know why, but a fierce panic grips me and my head whirls with the possibility of losing her. It shakes me to the core.

If what that Aris fucker said is true, then we're all in trouble. I witnessed some of it in the way the warehouse seemed to rock on its foundation without her batting an eye. With power that chaotic and dangerous…if she fell into the wrong hands…

"We need to get her out of here," I bark hastily at Cassius and glance around for the best exit out of this shithole. The only open garage door will do, and I run for it with Eve cradled in my arms. Cassius is quick on my heels, leaping over the dead without a second look.

"What about Knox?" he asks as we burst out into the frigid night.

I cross the blacktop in a flash and search the darkness for any signs of our getaway car, finding none. Anger flares. "What about him?"

"What if he's still in there somewhere with that maniac?"

"He can figure things out for himself," I growl. "He's a goddamn horseman too." *Where the fuck is the car?*

I am going to kill our driver. This isn't the first time he hasn't followed directions, or has left us high and dry during a job. It will be his last though.

In the distance, I spot the black tinted SUV with its lights off across the parking lot and curse. That is not where he was supposed to meet us, but at least this time he is on the right street. Picking up my pace, I race over to it.

Cassius throws open my door first so I can hurry inside with Eve before he runs around and jumps into the front passenger seat. Since I'm not exactly small in any sense of the word, I lay her across the second row, with her legs over my lap; it's the only way we'll both fit.

"Eve!" a woman's shrill voice comes from the third row. Based on her wrinkles and gray-streaked red hair, it's clear she's older. And the way she's cradling a hand with a severed finger, I can put two and two together and figure out that this is Kat. Eve's boss and the one Franco kidnapped to get us to meet him.

"Is she okay?" Kat asks, leaning over the seat. When she reaches out to touch her, a possessive growl rumbles in the back of my throat. She flinches and plops back into her seat.

The driver is white-knuckling the steering wheel, body as rigid as stone, but despite seeing us rushing into the car covered in blood, he still hasn't moved a finger to get us out of there.

Rage rises up within me, but luckily for him, Cassius is the first to say something.

"Rápido!" he shouts, waving his hand in a "get going" motion. "Mush! Go!"

Finally, the driver throws the car in reverse.

I grab the car door and yank it closed, but when I peek out my window, more flames and black smoke come pouring out of every door and window in the place. Then, out stumbles Aris, holding his flaming sword in his hand. He glances around, stumbling like he's lost. Even when he glances right at us, he just stands there, doing nothing. What's wrong with him?

The driver and Cassius must see him soon because the car still hasn't moved and a curse slips past Cassius's lips.

"Do we fight?" he asks me, looking from Aris back to me.

I peer down at Eve, whose face hasn't regained any color, and my heart constricts into a tight ball. It's not like me to turn down a fight, but Aris is a kind of monster we haven't faced before. And I will not risk Eve's life on anything. "Not this time," I say. "We need to get her somewhere safe. If Knox can't finish off his fucking brother, then we will another day. Besides, look at him. He stares at us like he doesn't know us."

Cassius stares out the window at Aris. "It's like he's lost his mind. What the fuck?"

"Or he's lost his memories?" I suggest. "Spell might have gone haywire. Did you cast the spell right?"

"Fuck yes I did. But we're not exactly dealing with a normal supe here."

I stare down at Eve, my chest squeezing. "Right now, we need to go."

Cassius slaps the back of the driver's headrest to snap him out of his fear. "You heard the man! What the fuck are you waiting for? Step on it!"

Wheels screech and spin in place, but suddenly we're flying backward. Kat's thrown in her seat and frantically searches for the seatbelt as the SUV's spinning around toward the darkened street. My gaze stays trained on the godlike man limping toward us. I'm waiting for an attack. Some supernatural, herculean move to stop us, but it never comes. Unexpectedly, he stops in the middle of the lot and only stares at us.

Stranger still is the look on his face. The rage and cockiness he displayed before is gone. What's left can only be described as a...deep *confusion*.

Squinting, he looks up at the sky and then scans the lot again, as if he has no idea where he is.

But that can't be right.

When the SUV swings around a corner, I lose sight of him completely, but I still stare out the back window in case he snaps out of it and decides to follow.

He doesn't.

"Cassius..." I start, glancing over my shoulder at

him. He's facing back, searching the darkened windows too. "What exactly was that spell meant to do again?"

Brows knitting together, he replies quickly, "Banish whoever was in the circle. It's always worked before."

"Maybe it had a different outcome for Aris because of what he is?"

"Hmm…that's my thought," he says. "It is fucking weird how he's not chasing after us right now. The way the bastard was before, you'd think he'd put up more of a fight."

My thoughts exactly.

A small groan snaps my attention to the blonde woman laying beside me. She's covered in blood. Her face and neck are marked by cuts, and there's a nasty bruise forming on her cheek.

If she wasn't in so much danger right now, I'd jump out of the car, run back to that warehouse, and pummel Aris until he was nothing but a smear on the pavement. But she's what matters now.

First, I need to make sure she's okay.

After refusing to go to the hospital, we drop off the older witch at one of the other stripper's places by the harbor. I'm sure Eve would insist Kat get treated for her wounds, but I don't care enough to push the issue. Plus, there's no way I'm allowing a stranger into our Tower. Not with the Spades and Aris still a very real threat.

Cassius's spell may have been enough to stun Aris

for the time being, but who knows how long that will last on a horseman? When he comes to, he'll be right on our tails again.

And coming after Eve.

The ride home is a quiet and tense one, but luckily it's also quick. The moment we pull into the underground garage and park the SUV, Eve jolts awake, scrambles to throw open the door, and vomits all over the concrete. The sour, pungent scent sucker-punches me in the nose instantly.

Cassius laughs. "At least she was smart enough to save the leather interior."

Her entire body convulses as she spews more bile out the door.

At the same time, Taliah throws open the heavy metal door and comes rushing over. As she rounds the car and spots Eve, she stops short.

"This is new," Cassius says as he hops out of the passenger seat. "Usually, you have to come out here after a job to patch one of us up before we bleed out. Never had to clean puke before."

She flinches in disgust. "I'm not sure which is worse, honestly."

Breathing heavily, Eve wipes her mouth with the back of her hand and glares daggers at Cassius. "Shut... the fuck...up."

He clasps his chest to feign surprise. "So mean! Even after we helped you save your boss and dropped her off at your friend, Dori's."

Her head perks up at that. "Kat's at Demi's? Why didn't she go to the hospital? Her finger—"

"That's what she wanted," I answer plainly.

She looks at me from over her shoulder, her gaze still full of fire. "You shouldn't have listened to her. She needs to be seen by a doctor."

"She's old enough to make that decision for herself."

"Ancient," Cassius adds with a chuckle.

"Here, let me help you," Taliah says in an attempt to pacify the situation. Trying to maneuver around the vomit puddle, she holds the car door open and takes Eve by the arms. Cassius reaches in too, but as she steps out, she loses her footing and almost falls.

"I gotcha." Cassius snatches her around the waist and pulls her up, but Taliah stumbles right into the puke.

"Oh, come on!" she shouts at her ruined heels, more aggravated than disgusted, which isn't too shocking. She has handled us in pretty battered up states. And she's had to *dispose* of some bodies for us in a pinch. She's seen worse. "These were new!"

"Sorry..." Eve croaks out weakly.

"We'll replace them." I climb out of the car. I'm about to walk over to take Eve from Cassius, but she's already shoving against him to let her go. He does so begrudgingly.

"I have legs, you know," she snaps.

He grins. "And a wicked mouth."

Ignoring him, she glances around the garage. "Where's Knox?"

He pauses, no doubt wondering how much he should tell her. After a long moment, he answers— surprisingly—with the truth, "We don't know."

"You don't—don't know?"

"Knox can take care of himself," I interject.

"He *is* Death after all," Cassius adds.

Eve snorts. "And your friend."

That takes both me and Cassius back. Friend might be a strong word for what Knox is to me. Hell, I'm not sure *friendship* could describe any of our relationships. We've always just worked well together. Had the same need for revenge and power. Our powers were matched in a way—we were all untouchable, or at least, we used to be. The only person I'd ever let close to me was Saxon, and that's what killed him.

Saxon was the one who kept us together. Without him, we were only business associates at best.

Using the silence to her advantage, Taliah quickly grabs Eve by the arm and guides her toward the security door. We follow behind them. After scanning her access card to unlock the door, she helps her through.

Another scan at the elevator and those doors roll open too, so we can all pile into the cramped space. The cart speeds past most of the floors, heading directly for the upper levels where we live. Being our assistant, Taliah is one of the select few who have access to our personal spaces. There aren't many people we can trust, for obvious reasons, and although our contract with the young woman has been brief, she's proven herself loyal and useful. Never questions anything, does what she's told, is usually seen but not heard—everything those in this line of work want from their associates.

When the doors open again, revealing our grand foyer, Eve lets her help her out of the elevator without a fuss, and I start to wonder if having Taliah around can be good for another reason.

For Eve.

"I'm going to get her cleaned up and taken care of," Taliah says and draws Eve closer. "The poor girl needs some TLC after whatever it is she went through, I'm sure."

Cassius glances at me with an arched brow, waiting for my word.

"She needs to come with us," I reply and pull back my aching shoulders. I would kill for a full steak dinner right now, with all the trappings. Shifting to my alternate forms always expends a lot of my energy, which leaves my stomach empty. As much as I know we all need to decompress after everything, there are a lot of things we have to discuss first. Like Eve's powers, her past, and how Aris ties into all of this.

And—of course—what the fuck we're supposed to do next.

Eve's eyes widen.

"Can it wait?" Taliah asks. "You saw what happened downstairs. She's so weak, she can hardly—"

"You're not here to inject your opinion, Taliah," I bite out, my anger growing. The message seems to get across though because she clamps her lips shut.

"She's right," Eve says. "I'm exhausted."

"We're all tired."

"Drac…" Cassius starts, sympathy in his tone. It only seems to piss me off more. "Maybe this can wait—"

"Wait until Aris comes barging through that door?" I

bellow, making Taliah wince. Eve, though, just stares me down.

I steel myself. Doesn't she realize how much danger she's in? How much danger we all are in with her here? Every second could be ticking down to another attack, to our deaths.

But even knowing all this, looking at her standing off with me, not giving in, and covered in scrapes and deep purple bruises, I feel my fury dissolving. I want to be in Taliah's place, comforting her, fighting *for* her. Not against her. I want to care for her, wash her, tend to her. And the notion rocks me to the core.

Things are changing between us, and I'm not sure I'm ready for that.

My shoulders fall, defeated. "Fine," I say despite my better judgment. "But you will be in the living room in forty-five minutes. Not a second later."

Eve's about to say something more, but Taliah quickly steers her down the hallway toward her bedroom before she can make anything worse.

Good. She needs to learn that my kindness is rare and practically nonexistent. She needs to take it and run.

When she and Taliah disappear and the bedroom door slams shut, I march into the living room and run my fingers through my hair. Over and over until my scalp burns and blood colors my nails.

"So." Clapping once, Cassius strides into the room and looks around. "We've pissed off a lot of people. That's nothing new. But this is the first time we've fucked with a god. What do we do?"

"Aris isn't a god," I reply shortly. "He can die. Just like all of us."

Cassius plops himself on the couch and stretches his legs out across the cushions. "Except there's only one weapon in all of creation that can take him out. And said weapon is currently MIA right now with wherever the fuck Knox is."

"He'll come back."

"You sure about that?"

"For Death, he's hard as fuck to kill."

Cassius sighs and drapes a hand dramatically over his head. "I can't believe everything he had been telling us about Aris and the stupid blade was true. And here I thought he was just a sociopath with murderous tendencies. Some kind of shadow manipulator or something," he says. "But all that hullabaloo about being a horseman and his scythe…it was all true."

"At least we know he's not a liar."

"That's for fucking sure." He chuckles but it's short lived. "So, when it comes to the fire-breathing bastard, we're stuck until Knox comes back. Hopefully with his blade in hand."

I grind my teeth. It very much seems that way, and I hate it.

"The Black Spades are easy pickings though. Although, I doubt they'll be crawling out of their holes anytime soon, now that their numbers are down. We killed a lot of them today," he goes on.

"There's always more. They're like rats," I reply.

"Or roaches."

That is a better comparison by far. Especially for

Franco, that coward. He ran for the hills the second he saw an opening and left his guys to be slaughtered.

Suddenly the balcony doors fly open and a rush of freezing night air floods the Tower.

"What the fuck!" I hear Cassius shout behind me as he scrambles to his feet.

Expecting Aris, my Apex beast roars, my primal side unleashing, ready to take on whatever form I need to send his ass hurtling over the railing to the streets below, but when a black mist comes swirling inside, it's clear it's not Aris who has come to visit.

It's Knox.

He transforms in a millisecond, the ghost shadow solidifying faster than a blink until a man stumbles across the room and right into the back of the opposing couch. Gasping for breath, he shoves himself off it, clumsily backpedaling until his back hits one of the columns. His dark hair is soaked and blood drips from his face and clothes all over the rug. In his hand is the Mortem Blade, also shining crimson.

"Knox!" Cassius moves toward him cautiously. "You okay, man? You're acting like you've been hitting the bottle."

Knox's head snaps up, his irises and pupils consumed by darkness.

"Oh shit," Cassius snaps and shifts back a step.

My energy hovers on the surface, leaving goosebumps along my arms. I'm ready to shift at a moment's notice if I have to—if for some reason, Knox has become rabid, the enemy.

A tense moment of silence stretches between us.

Knox's chest heaves with every labored breath, and his skin is so pale, I can clearly see the blue outlines of his veins underneath the surface.

He looks like a monster. Like something Dr. Frankenstein dug up and couldn't quite get right when he attempted to put him together.

"Where's...Eve..." He sucks in a breath and exhales between each word.

I step toward him, my heart pounding as another burst of protectiveness courses through my veins. "Not here," I say.

His nostrils flare—a gesture I recognize when a shifter or animal is trying to sniff their prey out—and he whirls for the door. "Her room."

I know his sense of smell isn't like mine, but he's a predator nonetheless. In a different way. He must be sensing her dark magic or whatever connection they have—if what Aris says is true and she is his daughter. They might not be related through blood, but that would mean she and Aris share the same cosmic energy. He might be able to track her that way.

Doesn't matter. There's no way I'm going to let him touch her.

Cassius is on the same page. He sprints with unnatural speed to stop Knox from getting any further. "Woah, Knox. Slow down. We're all wound up from what happened, but let's not do anything we're going to regret here."

He holds up his curved knife, its blade pointed at Cassius's chest. "Move." He growls the word.

The demon's eyes narrow on him, unafraid. "You gonna kill me, Knox? Me?"

His grip tightens on the Mortem Blade's handle. "That's why I'm telling you…to move."

"We are here to talk about this," I reply, which draws his attention over his shoulder to me. "To figure this out. Together."

"She is an abomination," he says.

"That's a bit harsh," Cassius replies.

"My kind isn't meant to breed with humans. For the longest time, we weren't even supposed to interact with them."

"But *you* interact with them. With us," I say.

"I didn't have a choice," he snaps. "Aris wanted my blade. Knowing I am the only creature in existence who could kill him, he wanted that power and sought out my scythe. We fought. He slaughtered my horse, and I was left in this realm with no way to return to my own."

He's told us all this before, but back then, we thought it was the rambles of a madman. Now, after finding out what Knox and Aris really are—horseman of the apocalypse—it makes more sense.

"Creating Eve must be another way Aris seeks to shift power solely to him. Creating another horseman, even partly so, disturbs the balance of nature." This time Knox turns fully to me, his inky eyes locking with mine. "Because of it, her power is unstable. She can end up killing this entire planet, this universe, if we don't destroy her first. And if Aris gets to her—"

"We're not going to let any of that happen," Cassius goes on. "None of it."

"You're thinking with your baser instincts, with your dicks!" he shouts.

He may be speaking the truth about a few things. The strange pull I have for Eve does seem to be primal, sexual, at least on some level. And Cassius appears to be smitten with her, too. She is an attractive woman. But I'm also trying to look at this from a different angle.

If Eve is as powerful as Knox claims, maybe we can use her to solidify our position on top again. A Death horseman, a Daughter of Chaos, an Apex predator, and a Hell demon. No one could touch us. We'd be feared and respected by every gang, every soul, in the country. Fuck, the world. We could expand. We could give Eve everything she could ever want and more. The Kings of Eden could finally be the gang Saxon and I had always dreamed it could be.

As dangerous as Eve may be, we can't kill her yet. Not when there's still so much we have to know about her and this power she possesses. And how we can use it to our advantage.

She can be our ultimate weapon.

Knox's dark hair spills over his face and his eyes bulge with anger. "Now, move before I cut you down where you stand. The woman must die."

Then a new scent hits my nose, a delicate, floral one of vanilla and lavender. I spin to see Eve standing by a nearby column with new clothes on and her hair still wet from a shower. The cuts on her cheek and forehead have been bandaged, and some tape and gauze peek out from under her sleeve. Taliah's beside her, looking horrified that they've been caught spying on the conversation.

Knox's gaze lands on them, too, more specifically on Eve, and in a flash, the black is replaced by the normal hazel we're used to. His shoulders drop instantly, and his blade falls to his side.

Looks like Cassius and I aren't the only ones affected by her—as much as Knox wants to deny it.

"You want to kill me?" Eve begins. Despite her voice being soft, her words sound like a gunshot in the otherwise silent room.

She crosses the living room with quick steps, standing in front of me to face off with Knox head on. Then, she does something even more shocking. She jabs a pointed nail into his chest.

Into *Death's* chest, and leans in close.

"Do it," she whispers. "Do it, Knox, because every second I've been alive has been nothing but utter chaos, and I'm tired of trying to hold all the pieces together to create some semblance of normal. So do it. Kill me."

He doesn't move. None of us do. We're all too confused and stunned by her blatant wish for death to grant it. Even Knox.

"Do it!" she screams in his face, her entire body jerking forward. The walls shudder all around us, and the floor feels like it's swaying under my feet. Plaster rains down on us, and when I look up, jagged cracks are crawling along the ceiling.

Fuck, she's going to bring the Tower down if she keeps it up.

Cassius and I silently inch closer. Knox only blinks at her.

"Kill me, you pathetic asshole! Or are you a coward? DO IT! KILL ME!"

Slowly, he lifts the Mortem Blade.

I seize Eve from behind and haul her backward before Knox decides to actually take her up on her absurd wish. She kicks and bucks against me, but I hold her tight. Then I remember Taliah is still there watching.

"Get out," I bark at her. That's all she needs; she runs for the elevator. Who knows what she's already heard about Aris and horsemen and whatnot. I'm sure I'm going to have to explain some things after all this, but I can't worry about that now. We have more important shit on our plate.

Eve throws her head back, nailing me in the nose. Colors burst before my eyes as the pain spikes through my skull and I release her, growling. Not broken, luckily. But it fucking hurts just the same.

Fucking cheap shot.

"I don't understand you." Her hardened gaze sweeps the room to each of us, but at least the quaking around us has stopped. "Any of you. One second you want nothing to do with me, the next you want to kill me." She lingers on Knox. Surprisingly, he sheaths the Mortem Blade. "And now what? You're trying to protect me?"

"Of course, we are," Cassius replies with a shrug. "If we didn't want to keep you around, you wouldn't be here. It's that simple."

"Nothing with you three is ever simple," she bites back, but her early anger seems to be leaving her.

Cassius's cocky smirk sneaks across his lips. "That's fair."

She sighs heavily and moves to the couch Cassius had stretched across earlier. "Does anyone have a plan to stop this psycho?"

I shake the last of the pain out of my nose. "First, I think you should tell us about your mother. And how Aris is connected to you."

"You don't actually believe that lunatic do you? There's no way he's actually my father."

"Then who is your real father?" Cassius asks. "Do you know him?"

She pauses. "Well, no. But I just assumed he was some deadbeat. My mom always acted like he was."

"Aris violated your mother," Knox says bluntly. "It's the only explanation."

"Violated? As in raped?"

He nods once. "Aris sees the living as beneath him. He wouldn't show her respect or mercy."

Eve shrinks back into the couch, as if the news has rocked her to the core.

I don't understand why. When I had done my research on Eve, I'd found out her and her mother had a strained relationship. Her mother had kicked her out at an early age, and the two haven't spoken since. Yet, Eve seems crushed by Knox's news and is silent, her hands clutched in her lap.

"Eve," Cassius starts gently and comes to sit beside her, "you might not believe it, but we are here to keep

Aris away from you. To keep you safe. So we need you to tell us anything you know about your mother and Aris and your powers. It can help us protect you from him."

She glances up at him, eyes glistening with pending tears. "I don't know anything about him. I don't. All I know is that she's human, so I always assumed I'd gotten this…this…*curse* of a power from my father. But I'd never known who he was. She hated me for what I was. Hated me."

As the tears begin to slide down her cheeks, the urge to reach over and hold her against me takes hold, leaving me sweaty and shaky. This isn't a normal feeling for me. It's concerning.

Instead, Eve leans into Cassius, who wraps an arm around her and brings her close.

"Hey now, family's complicated, right? Shit, don't even get me started on mine and our issues," Cassius attempts to joke, but is ignored. He slides a finger under her chin to force her to look at him. "If that's all you know, that's all you know. It's fine. We can figure out the rest."

"Aris is weakened now," Knox says. "Whatever spell you did disoriented him."

"It was meant to banish his soul to Hell," Cassius says. "Instead it seemed to make him forget who we are. At least for now."

"He doesn't have a soul to banish."

"That fucking explains it."

"But with him weakened, that means now's our time

to attack," he goes on. "I still have my blade. I can kill him."

"He probably knows you'll be coming after him. He'll be hiding out," I say.

Knox's hand rests on the hilt of the dagger on his belt. "We can track him down. We have to kill him first, before he regains his memories and full power. This is our only chance, while your spell disabled him."

"And what about me?" Eve pipes up from the couch. "You said it yourself, Knox. What I am…it's unstable. My power, I don't know how to control it. I don't want to hurt anyone."

"We'll figure that out, too," I assure her, hating the pain in her voice.

"There can't be five horsemen," Knox interjects bluntly. I glare at him, but he continues, not getting the hint. "It's unnatural. We don't know what this could mean for the natural order of things. The world could collapse on itself."

"It hasn't so far," I growl.

"He's right, though," she says. "There can't be five. I have always felt this wrongness inside me, like me being here isn't…right."

Sounds like something a fucked-up mother would say to a child she regretted having. Hearing it for most of her life has Eve believing it to be true.

"Then we'll kill Aris," Cassius offers. "There. Simple. Then there will be four again. See, math can be easy."

"We just have to find him first," I reply. And something tells me that finding where War is hiding may end up being just as tricky as killing the apocalyptic bastard.

CHAPTER THREE

EVE

I'm going to throw up again.

Stumbling out onto the balcony, I pause by the railing and stare up into the stormy sky where the cool breeze swipes over my face, taking my tears with it.

The thought of War—Aris—being my father, of him raping my mother, runs through my mind like a bulldozer, ripping me to shreds. With it comes a sickness churning in my gut about the secrets of my life I'd never known.

All these years, my mother never told me a thing about my dad, yet she lived with the hatred of what he did to her.

Oh, God. Of what I represented.

The man who forced himself on her.

Tears tumble down my face and each breath sharpens in my chest. I wipe my cheeks, remembering all the hatred she harbored toward me. No matter what I did, I was never good enough. Never fucking enough.

Now I understand why. But it doesn't excuse her, and it sure as hell doesn't change the resentment I still hold toward her. I was a damn child, and she treated me like trash.

Yet, the truth of who I really am has irrevocably shattered my world. I shiver at the notion, hating the idea deep down to the pit of my stomach.

Heartache flares in my chest the longer I think about the repercussions, not to mention the confusion of what this now means for me.

One thing's for sure. I hate Aris and want nothing to do with him. I want him dead. Even if he is my father...I don't fucking care.

My knuckles turn white from how hard I hold onto the balcony railing, and I lower my gaze to the bustling city below, thinking about how I got to this situation. How bad the attack on the warehouse had gone. On the bright side, we rescued Kat. But as much as I tell myself to be happy, I'm struggling.

I sigh, and pain flickers inside me once more, deepening as I recall her locked in the cage, remembering her severed finger being sent to us.

Since finding out we dropped Kat off at Demi's place, I'd been filled with guilt. I was the reason she had been targeted in the first place. She would have been better off not ever having met me at all.

It's the story of my life apparently. And now three Kings won't let me out of their sights. For the first time since arriving at their tower-of-monsters, I think I'm safer here.

I want to cry at the thought. I had tried so hard to

escape, and now I'm resigned to the fact that something more terrifying is out to get me.

That whole "better the devil you know" shit is starting to grate on my nerves because I doubt I'm better off. I'd been living blissfully unaware of my past until Franco pulled that shit at the club, and now look at me.

I'm royally fucked.

My father is a horseman of the apocalypse. I can't get that part out of my head.

So, what does that make me? The horseman's daughter of the apocalypse? It definitely explains the strange powers I possess. My attempt to laugh comes out strangled. If I thought my life was chaotic before, things have just exploded to universal proportions of insanity.

That's when the strike of footsteps behind me has me reluctantly turning around.

Knox is practically flying out on the balcony, chaos flaring in his eyes. He's pissed...that's the first thought that ignites in my mind. He's pissed at me.

"You," he starts, but there's something in his accusing voice that irritates me.

I draw in a shuddering breath and give him my best sarcastic glare as I square my shoulders. "What do you want, Knox? Or should I call you, Uncle Death? God, we're related by blood." I almost puke in my mouth at the words, thinking of how attracted I've been to him. A blood relative. Shit! Thank the gods we never had sex.

His expression twists into something more serious than I've ever seen him. He once stared at me with molten stars in his eyes…now they looked ready to hurl daggers into my heart.

"Don't fucking calling me that," he snarls, closing the distance between us. "And don't worry, little dove, we're not blood related. Aris and I are mere brothers by the forces that summoned us to power."

His words struck a chord with me that we're not related after all. I should be relieved, but I'm too busy trying to work out why he's so mad at me.

He stands inches away, stealing all my personal space and growling in my face, "I should have trusted my instincts from the beginning, that you were my enemy and needed to die."

My mouth drops open and I don't care that he sees my shock. "Fuck you. You can threaten all you want, but as we saw before, you won't kill me. You're all talk," I snap back, completely taken aback by his attack. I shove my hands into his chest. "Get the hell off me."

He doesn't budge, but stands there unaffected by my push. The guy is huge, a monstrous giant and just as strong, and I won't deny he's slightly terrifying. Yet, I'm too annoyed to put up with his hissy fit.

He surprises me by grabbing my wrists and forcing my arms behind my back as he towers over me. There's disdain on his face, and he's glaring at me like I *am* his enemy. He's insane.

I try to find my words but I'm too busy pulling against him as he pins me against the balcony railing. One shove, and I'll fall over.

"It changes nothing, but I need you out of my fucking head," he snarls harshly, squeezing his grip on my wrists to the point of pain, and presses up against me. My breasts are crushed to his chest, and I hear the way his breath hitches in response.

Wild, black hair flairs around Knox's beautiful face. The shadow of growth on his square jawline always makes me want to run my fingers over it, even when I am furious with him. But with the way he's staring at me like a psychopath, I half expect him to whip out his switchblade and wave it in my face. He doesn't go anywhere without it, and the asshole is unpredictable.

Black-rimmed hazel eyes pierce into me, studying my face with the intensity of a scientist examining a new microorganism. On top of that, I can't help but be enveloped by the confused emotions he stirs in me. Hatred. Fury. Arousal.

Hell, what's wrong with me?

"You've got me so angry, so turned on," he growls. "I hate you, and that makes me want to fuck you harder, to give you pain. To feel your pussy stretched over my cock as I ram into you. To have you scream with agony."

I gasp at his words, my pussy pulsing with a need I shouldn't be feeling for the monster who wants to hurt me, to kill me.

I whine from his restraints, well aware that if we remain like this, I'll give in and he'll fuck my brains out. And the bad thing is that I know I'll enjoy it. Then I'll regret it as he *will* hurt me. And I have no intention of lowering my guard around him. So, I drive my knee right up to where the sun don't shine. He shifts his hips out of the way, but he's not quick enough as I still catch him on the edge of his precious jewels.

He groans, his face pinching with pain, and his misery makes me smile, especially the part where he releases me.

"What the fuck's your problem?" I practically shout at him as I slip out of his grasp and move toward the glass doors of the apartment.

"You're his daughter," he groans, pausing me in my steps. "That fucker, Aris, destroyed everything I had, and he won't stop until I'm dead. Except, he has no idea that I will smash this world into pieces and put everyone's lives at risk, including mine, to eliminate him. And you are his offspring, the only thing he might care about. And that makes you my enemy. My chance to make him suffer."

"Are you delusional?" My hands shake as I turn around to face him. He's hunched over, one hand clasping the railing in a death grip, his other cupping his groin.

"Fuck this mortal body," he gasps from the pain. It only makes me wish I struck him harder. I want to know what he looks like when he has tears in his eyes—that's how much he's got me seething.

"You sound like a fucking martyr." My voice quivers with rage. "Aris wants me dead as well, not to hold a damn family reunion. So, what's your plan, then? Kill me? What will that achieve?"

"Satisfaction," he says, more emotion and conviction behind his words than I expect.

Something comes over me. Maybe it's fury, or that I've just had enough of everyone's bullshit. But I march toward him because, evidently, his threats are enough to send me over the edge.

This time, I step up into his face, trying my best not to tremble. "You don't scare me, Knox. If you really wanted me dead, you would have done it already, but instead you threaten me with words. I'm not the enemy here. Maybe *you* are."

He smirks in response. "You sure have some brass balls for a little girl to talk to me that way."

Cocky asshole. His stare is so severe, I wonder if he can see my soul. My chest heaves for each breath and a shudder races up my spine. The look on his face is the one I'd seen before when he tortures his victims.

I step back instantly.

Where his previous movements had been manic, they suddenly become calculated and lighting fast.

One second, I'm recoiling, and the next, he's got me flung over the railing, fisting my clothes so tightly across my chest that I'm suspended mid-air. I feel weightless, carried so easily that it terrifies me. I can barely suck in a breath.

I half-scream from the shock and terror. Gripping onto his rock-hard arm with my life depending on it, I yell in his face, "Are you fucking insane? Pull me back." I hate how frantic I sound and how my legs are just dangling over open air.

"How about we start again," he says. I'm starting to feel lightheaded. "You are my enemy, little dove, and now I have to correct my mistakes. But you're right. Killing you is too hasty. Let's start with you telling me about your power. Every horseman has unique abilities. Tell me more about yours."

I suck in a raspy breath, shaking, unable to think straight, but my head screams to use my power. But focusing is the last thing I can do as my synapses snap with panic, my brain screaming at me to get to safety. "You psychopath, pull me back." My fingers dig into his arm for purchase as fear lifts every hair on my body.

"Trust me, Eve, you don't want to push me. Talk, and I'll consider sparing your life."

"You're drunk on vengeance, asshole. You're a fucking monster," I snap, breathing raggedly.

My head spins, and I keep telling myself not to look down. *God, please don't look down.*

Of course, that's exactly what I do, and the world spins dizzyingly at how high up I am...how tiny the road is, the people, the cars. Dread slides over my skin like razor blades.

"Knox, what the fuck!" Cassius shouts, and I snap my head up.

I want to cry out loud because seeing Cassius rushing onto the balcony is the best sight in the whole freaking world.

Knox wrenches me back onto the balcony like I weigh nothing, and when my feet hit the concrete, I fall to my knees, gasping for air.

I'm so enraged, so shaken, that it takes me a few moments to gain composure and look up. But when I finally recover, Cassius and Knox are in a shouting match, shoving each other. And just as quick, Knox storms back into the penthouse.

Cassius has me on my feet in seconds and pulled into his arms before I can catch my breath. I swallow hard, eager to be as far from the balcony as possible. So, I eagerly accept his help to get me back inside.

"That fucking asshole," I mumble under my breath.

"I promise, it will turn out alright, even if it doesn't feel like it like yet," Cassius reassures me, his powerful arms wrapped around me and guiding me to the couch.

Trembling, I turn around to face him, still disbelieving what happened and how easily I could have just died. How panic made me freeze when it came to drawing on my own power.

I stare at the gorgeous demon holding onto me, one of the Kings, with his beautiful golden skin and his sandy hair buzzed along the sides. Notches have been etched in his eyebrows, and they always draw my stare to his hypnotic steel-blue eyes.

Even now, I find myself mesmerized by him, almost forgetting the shitstorm on the balcony. Forgetting would be nice, but the memories come rushing back, and I pull free from Cassius's arms because is he any safer? Are any of the Kings?

"I don't see how anything can be normal again. For all I know, I'll be long dead by Knox before Aris even gets his memories back and comes for me."

Cassius's lips pinch tightly. "Gorgeous, you need to know that Knox has been broken for a long time. He's got some dark shit relating to Aris. He's been stuck on Earth, biding his time until he gets his revenge. And now he's going to become a bigger pain in my ass than I thought possible with Aris in town. But trust me, I'll make sure the prick never hurts you again."

I don't know how to feel. Everything about Knox

hurts my head. The crazy love/hate relationship we have going on might very well be the end of me.

Cassius cups the side of my face, distracting me from my thoughts. His large palm is hot and tender against my skin. He smells so wonderful, it leaves me slightly dizzy. Like fresh rain and something that is all him, masculine, and underneath it all is a smoky smell. His scent melts my knees. Around him, I find myself losing control. He makes me forget myself, and his eyes promise me safety in a world drowning in darkness.

"Cassius." I try to find my words, but his name slips out a little breathy.

"What is it, gorgeous? I'm here for you." He reaches out to pull me back into his arms.

But everything is spinning in my head. Too much has happened lately, and these heavy emotions for the Kings are just confusing me. Needing to get a hold of myself, I retreat from Cassius, holding onto his stormy gaze as uncertainty dances over my face. "I-I can't do this," I say.

I turn on my heels and rush out of there, running right for my room, my prison, ignoring his calls after me.

For a long time, I thought the world was broken around me. That I was cursed with bad luck. But now I'm starting to wonder if the problem has been me all along. Because perhaps the Kings aren't the only broken people in this tower.

CHAPTER FOUR

KNOX

I'm losing it.

I always knew that I wasn't right in the head. Not after the fucking stunt Aris pulled so long ago that trapped me here on Earth, but now all the things I've been dreading are become reality.

The fucker Aris finally found me. And the one woman who actually pushed past my defenses isn't who she says she is.

Just fucking great.

I pace up and down in my den, the Mortem Blade tight in my grip.

I never should have let her get close to me. I was already balancing on an edge, already close to losing my mind. And now, no excuses I made to myself justify my actions because I let myself start to fall for my enemy.

I promised to kill Aris, and that includes his family… that includes Eve. It gutted me to hear her whimpers when I held her over the balcony railing, taking every inch of strength to hold her out there, so how the fuck am I supposed to end her?

Weak. That's what I've become. And maybe it was time Eve saw the real me, and for me to remember who the hell I was. A motherfucking horseman of the apocalypse. And instead of her staring at me with those big doe eyes, she needed to fear me. Then it'll be easier to finish her, to make Aris suffer.

A guttural groan from across the room draws my attention. The pitiful sound has me lifting my gaze to the fucker I'd dragged off the streets and into my morgue after finding him stabbing a blade into a local shopkeeper to steal his money.

I have no clue who he is, but he's a shifter. I know by the wet fur stink filling my room. He's not one of our men. Right now, I need to spill blood. To look into his bulging, terrified eyes and tell myself this is what it'll feel like to take out Aris.

Tucking my Mortem Blade into the back of my pants, I crack my neck and go to him with bare hands.

The shifter trembles violently, like he's about to shift. He writhes against the chains pinning his arms to the wall, his screams swallowed by his gag.

He's going to be sorry we ever crossed paths.

I am Death. Everyone fears me. And I'm fucking tired of hiding.

I throw myself at him, his eyes huge with terror. Fists raised, teeth bared, I can barely contain myself.

The present fades in and out, and with the darkness in my mind feathering at the edges with fury, my past with Aris crashes over me.

"You sonofabitch!" Aris growls, the bright amber in his eyes growing brighter, shallower with irritation. "You're a greedy asshole, you know that? Now, hand over the fucking Mortem Blade."

My shoulders rear back, yet his demand shouldn't be a surprise. We've had this conversation dozens of times already. But, over time, Aris has changed and grown more jealous of power, more aggressive toward me. As the horseman of War, he embraces those traits naturally, but this is something else. Something cruel and vindictive.

I'd been assigned as the keeper of the knife, to ensure when all four horsemen are together, we yield the unimaginable collective power of the blade. So, what Aris asks will lead to dissension within our group. To death and chaos.

"We're a team, or have you forgotten?" I snap, close to losing my shit.

He chuckles, throwing his head back, but there's nothing except a harsh, brutal glare in his eyes.

I blink, trying to focus, as the sun shines blinds me from behind him in the open field, because of course he'd asked me to meet him out here in the middle of fucking nowhere, alone.

"Why is it only you who gets to guard the Mortem Blade? If we're equal, then we take turns. So, give it to me." He sticks out his hand, palm up, fingers curling. His tongue darts out of his mouth and licks his lips.

His greed baffles me. We've faced monumental battles together, dealt with gods, faced endless loss, and now he's turning on his own kind for the blade?

"It stays with me. I am the horseman of Death, so back the fuck off. I won't repeat myself," I threaten, anger flaring through my chest that we even have to have this conversation again.

"Fuck you." His words morph into a harsh snarl. "The blade will be mine."

There's no pause before the fucker lunges forward and comes at me with the speed of a tornado. Rage twists his face, a blur of red fog trailing behind him, his eyes burning like flames, his sharp teeth showing.

My stomach hardens as reality rattles through me. The truth is, jealousy had made this horseman into my enemy. So, what would a powerful weapon like the Mortem Blade be used for when wielded by someone who lost his grip on his reality?

Regardless, I attack Aris, fury gripping me by the throat and not letting go. The man I once considered close enough to be my brother has turned on me, and I'm fucking furious. I charge, fury rippling down my spine.

We clash with a terrible blow, the boom explosive and rattling the very foundation of the cosmos.

I go feral, fists and teeth tearing into the horseman. I'd forgotten what it was like to face my mortality but now, at the hands of another horseman who seeks the Mortem Blade, my end could come swiftly. Another reason, I can't trust Aris.

I see only red, only fury, only the ugly bastard, head-butting me. Hitting the ground with a thump, the sound resonates, and I know it'll ripple across the universe. I move with renewed speed, throwing myself into the air and plunging back down right on top of Aris. He crumbles beneath me, and I slam my fists into his face, over and over. I drive him into the ground, unrelenting, and for the first time, I see dread in his eyes.

"Knox," he pleads, which is pathetic, and still it catches me off guard just long enough for the asshole to jam a knife I hadn't seen him holding right under my ribs.

It sinks into me, burning like fire, and I curse, the pain excruciating. Normal blades do nothing to our kind except hurt like a bitch and distract us. Bastard.

With a powerful punch to my chest, I fly backward then hit the ground with an explosive thud. The ground beneath me splits open, sending cracks across the land. I can only imagine the horrendous earthquakes I'd just unleashed on so many worlds.

I barely have time to react. Aris lands on my chest, kneeling, grinning like a psychopath. "If you won't abide by my command, then I will break you and take the Mortem Blade for myself."

He lands a tremendous punch to my face. I groan as the world spins with me and a screaming ache cuts across my skull. It's only when I open my eyes, that I see the bastard getting up and gripping the Mortem Blade he must have stolen from my belt.

Rage curls in my gut, my muscles flexing, and I scramble up, throwing myself at him with a blood-curdling growl. I slam into him and drag him to the ground, and our fight turns vicious, hits faster and harder. We move quickly, attacking, my sights locked on the Mortem Blade.

"Your technique is improving, brother," he mocks me.

"Go fuck yourself. The blade isn't yours." That's when I crack my fist into his ribs, and his flinch is just enough for me to snatch his fist and grasp my blade.

A jolt of electricity races through us, due to us both holding the weapon at once.

Suddenly, a brilliant flash of light blinds us, and the world literally breaks apart around us. The sky fades in color, darkness spreading across the heavens. I stumble across the trembling, splintering ground, opening up like a portal to Hell

But we never pause the battle, and it's only when we both lose our footing from the ground giving way beneath us that the blade slips out of Aris's grasp.

Everything seems to slow as I watch the most powerful weapon in the world hit the edge of the crevice, then bounce right into its depth.

Panic claws at me and I leap to my feet, then for good measure kick Aris in the gut. "Look what you've done, your fucking prick."

I whistle and in seconds, my steed, Time, appears. He's spectacular, the color of ash, rearing before me, his lengthy mane wild and blowing in the breeze. There's no time to waste, and I lunge to him before leaping up onto his back.

"Move," I command, tapping my heels to his side. "Follow the Mortem Blade." I point down to the widening crack in the ground in front of us. "Need to find it before I lose it forever."

Time turns to dive in, while I hold tightly to his mane. It's in that exact moment that my steed releases a painful groan, the kind of sound I'd never heard from him before. My insides clench.

I twist my head around to find Aris's sword sticking out of Time's side.

Blood pours from the wound, and my lungs scream for air as I bellow furious roar. Time and I are bound, he's been with me since my beginning. My friend, my supporter, my family.

Aris unceremoniously wrenches his sword free from my horse's side with a sickening grin.

"I will rip everything from you," he threatens. "I will track down the blade, then I'm coming for you." Behind him, his red steed materializes.

Then next thing I know, Time falls over the edge of the fissure, taking me with him, stealing my words.

And we plunge into darkness...

Head spinning, I growl with the memory that plagues me every fucking day. Aris turned on me, desperate to gain power over all the horsemen. But that's the problem, isn't it? I don't trust the prick to not take us all out. He's the reason I ended up on Earth as I chased to find the Mortem Blade and ultimately lay low to avoid him finding me again. Of course, most of that had everything to do with him killing my horse, Time, and trapping me here. Without my horse, I can't travel beyond this world.

For what he did, Aris is going to fucking suffer. I'll ruin him for taking time from me, for trying to kill me, for spawning Eve and making her my enemy! That last one pisses me off severely. An ache flares in my chest, and I swallow, then lick my lips, tasting shifter blood.

It's only then that my mind clears and I stare at the sucker in front of me that I remember where I am. The shifter I had been torturing remains chained on the wall, and it's close to impossible to recognize him. Blood flows in rivulets down his body, his chest cavity is pried open, his throat split in half. And those barren eyes remain open in pure shock.

Fuck me, but I had fun with him, didn't I? And yet, I barely remember doing it, lost in my own head. So much for that. Next one I'll pay attention and enjoy every damn bone I break, every slice I take from his body.

"You asshole," Cassius roars from behind me, distracting me from my handiwork.

I twist my head to stare at him over my shoulder.

The demon fills the doorway to the morgue, heaving for breath like a damn bear, fire burning in his hellish eyes.

"Fuck off," I snap in his direction, before turning back toward the sucker, figuring how to get rid of the body so I can go find myself a new victim to play with. I'm in a creative mood today.

Hard footfalls resonate behind me. I hate being disturbed. I clench my teeth and turn to meet the demon's gaze. "What the fuck do you want? Money? Tips on picking up a girl? Whatever it is, go fuck yourself."

The dick snatches me by the throat, moving so fast, I'm taken aback. Color me surprised. "I like this side of you better," I laugh in his face.

He slams my back to the wall, pinning me in place, his hand constricting around my throat this time. There's no fear in me, just frustration.

"What the hell is wrong with you?" he spits in my face. "I always knew you were broken, but I swear to all the darkness in the pits of Hell that I will make you a permanent fixture in the ocean if you don't pull your fucking cry-baby bullshit tantrum back up your ass."

I blink at this monstrous bastard, knowing instantly why he's furious, and I curl my lips into a grin. Speaking is impossible with the pressure he's got on my jugular, so I shove the heel of my hand right into his solar plexus. He gasps, releasing me as he smacks a hand to his chest to catch his breath.

"You're weak." I shove another arm against his shoulder. "You're letting yourself have feelings for that…that…*creature*. Having her in our home is a death sentence for all of us once Aris gets his memories back. He'll be drawn to her." I don't know when I started roaring, and I drive a fist into his belly.

He coughs, then comes at me, anger flashing behind his gaze. He pummels into me, his fists coming fast into my middle, and I laugh. Maybe this is what I crave, to be knocked out, to get all the fucking shit out of my head. To forget it all.

I don't fight back, just hold my arms out on either side of me and bellow a laugh. "Go your hardest. Nothing you do can hurt me. I've lost everything. I'm already damaged beyond anything you can do to me. And if you are smart, you'd heed my warning and we would eliminate the girl."

A muscle along his temple twitches, his fiery eyes narrowing. "You touch a hair on Eve, and I'll cut you into pieces then bury half of you in Hell so you can never be put together. You fucking understand me?"

"You like her that much, then? She'll be the end of all of us, and you're okay with that? Fascinating. You have no idea what Aris is capable of to get what he wants."

Cassius never answers. Not even in acknowledgment, but his fist comes flying and clips me dead center in the face. The piercing ache flaring from my nose and has my eyes tearing up. "You fucking bastard."

I stumble back.

"I won't warn you next time," Cassius snarls. "Back the fuck off from Eve. Don't blame her for your shit with Aris. She's not the reason you and him are warring."

"You have no idea what you're talking about." I reach up and hold my nose, then snap it back into place. I tense all over, grinding my jaw how much that hurts. But I show Cassius nothing. "Now get the fuck out of my face before you really piss me off, and not even Dracon will be able to save you."

Despite his cold glare, I catch the hard swallow as his Adam's apple moves. He knows the only reason I haven't killed him yet is because of my word to Dracon. But if he pushes me, I'll destroy him, and I'm in an especially stabby mood today.

"Get your fucking shit together, otherwise Dracon and I will do it for you." He storms out.

"Asshole."

I twist my attention back to the dead man in my room, while the agony for Eve I can't shake off tears through me, seeming to dissect right into my very soul. Sucking in a sharp breath, I leave the room, pushing away the darkness trying to engulf me.

I'm livid that Cassius's words are getting to me about Eve. Eliminating her will bring Aris pain, I know it will, but thinking of her awakens an excitement in me I've never felt before.

Fuck. This is why I need her out of my world because I fear if anyone is going to break me to the point of no return. It's Eve, my little dove.

EVE

I stand in the kitchen, holding the fridge door open and staring at the containers of premade meals. Dracon had arranged for the pantry and fridge to be filled with food for me, and he's even hired someone to make dishes for me. After the fiasco on the balcony with Knox yesterday, I've been overwhelmed by everything. Aris is out there—how long before he gains his memories back and comes for me? I feel trapped in the Tower, and yet I don't want to leave.

Staring at all the delicious food still doesn't make me hungry. I know I have to try to eat, and that Dracon and Cassius will protect me. Knox is a different story altogether and I hate how I still feel an attraction to him when he's a monster. The worst part is that my body still responds to him, it throbs when I think of him.

Sighing at how messed up my own mind is, I end up grabbing an apple from the counter and biting into its sweet, juicy flesh. Reality comes to me...what I feel for Knox is all about pleasure, offering me a moment to escape my worries and to let my fears fall aside. He offers me an escape, just like the other two Kings.

I can't ignore that my life is one huge messed-up tangle. No wonder I crave escape.

After a few more bites, I toss the core into the bin. I make my way out, heading back to my room when a dark figure appears in the hallway, blocking my path.

Knox.

My stomach clenches, and every hair on my body raises. I freeze.

He's dressed in all black—jeans and a long-sleeved tee—and his eyes are trained on me. I sense him tense in my presence.

When he steps out of the shadows, my breath catches. Despite everything, I still have to admit that he is beautiful. Especially when he's broody with shadows dancing across his face.

An awkward silence fills the space, and I say something because I apparently can't keep quiet. "Knox," I begin, my words and my breath increasing in speed. "I think it's best if we keep our distance."

He tilts his head to the side. "What makes you think I want anything else with you?" he questions dryly.

His response, and the way his upper lip curls, catches me off guard. Of course, it shouldn't, after the shit he pulled on the balcony, and yet it leaves me slightly startled.

I take a deep, shaky breath and stand up to him. "I'm not afraid of you, Knox. So, if you're scared that I might be more powerful than you, that is your problem." Of course, I'm lying through my teeth, but I'm still furious at him. With these men, I notice if I show my weakness, they walk all over me.

So, I brace myself for his reaction, my muscles tensing, but just as I finish speaking, he takes a long stride toward me. My heart jumps all the way up the back of my throat.

"Really?" he answers sarcastically, closing in.

Instinct has me retreating until my heels hit the wall

and I'm pinned in place. He slaps a hand to the wall over my shoulder, grinning down. The guy is huge, towering over me.

Seems I've amused him again, but when it comes to Knox, that's a dangerous thing. He sniffs, and that's when I spot a small trail of white powder around his nostrils, and am immediately reminded of Cassius inhaling cocaine back in the parking area of the party to control his demon.

"You're high?" I blurt, not sure I want to see a horseman go apeshit while floating on coke.

"It does shit-all for me. I snorted everything Cassius had and the most it did was tingle my nostrils. What a fucking waste, and makes me wonder if it even helps the demon or if it's all in his dumbass head."

"You're still pissed at the world, I see," I remark, not ready to show him any kind of weakness. Even this close to him, I'm proud of myself for standing up to him. But when he steps even closer, I smell his cologne…irresistible, seductive, and manly, with a hint of cedarwood. I've managed to remind myself I'm toying with actual Death, to not let my guard down. But now, a simple whiff of him has butterflies bursting free in my stomach.

"They say that everyone wants what they can't have," he begins, completely throwing me for a loop with his change of subject. "What do *you* want, little dove?"

"That's easy. I want you to get the hell off me and never cross paths with me."

"And do you know what I want?" he purrs, though there's something menacing behind the words that leave me slightly unsettled. Another saying comes to my mind, one about how the devil doesn't come to us with his horns and fangs, but rather, disguised as everything you've ever wanted. And right now, that's what Knox represents.

"Let me guess? To kill me and Aris, then you can live your blissful little life torturing anyone who crosses your path."

The corner of his mouth curls up deliciously, as does one of his thick eyebrows, and it's hard to deny how gorgeous this monster looks. He leans in, his hot breath on my ear sending shivers down my arms. "I'm trying to understand why a spectacular creature like you draws out my darkest desires, especially when you've been hiding behind illusions of who you really were. You're a wicked seductress. And just like Eve and her forbidden apple, the question becomes—will you be forgiven for your sin? Or is temptation too great and, before you know it, you've fallen?"

Breathless, my heart pounds hard in my chest, and my skin dimples from his breath on my neck. "Get off me," I finally say, finding my words, my hands pressing to his solid chest, which moves him not an inch.

"One bite is all it takes to remove you from existence," he whispers. He breathes in my scent, and I feel the feather-light touch of his lips on my neck. I dig my fingers into his chest, fisting his shirt, screaming in my head to push him away, and yet, in his presence, I want his darkness. I long to drown in it because I fear I'm a lot more similar to him than I want to admit.

Pulling back, his gaze drags up and down my body,

then looks into my eyes like they're piercing into my soul. His body pins me against the wall, leaving my knees weak and a fire flaring over me. Every single emotion funnels down to the lust he awakens in me. I remind myself I don't need him so I should fight him at every chance.

He needs to understand that I won't take his terror.

Yet, the combination of exhilaration and fear of what he promises stretches over my stomach with anticipation. I'm a masochist. That must be it, because who else has their palms sweating and underwear drenched at the same time?

Even under his cruel stare, I'm suffocating with desire.

His hard cock is poking me mercilessly in the stomach.

I gasp for air, and as I push against him, I clench my thighs.

Clearing my throat to sound somewhat normal and not reveal that my underwear is wet and clinging to me. "Y'know, you might do better focusing on eliminating Aris, instead of wasting your time on me. I can't help you, in any way."

His laugh takes me by surprise, and I feel him grinding his hardness against me gently, yet somehow also menacingly. He's still got both his hands pressed to the wall on either side of my head, and my attempt to shove him away this time is half-hearted, leaving me sick to my stomach how much I've let him influence me.

My face is flushed enough for him to see exactly the impact he has on me. The tension in the air thickens as we're locked in this insane embrace that smothers me with confusion.

"I wouldn't get too comfortable, little dove. Like I said, I'm still deciding if I should fuck you or kill you." His breath dances across my mouth as he threatens me. Then he pulls back abruptly and turns away. Not looking back at me, he strolls down the hall and turns a corner, vanishing.

Alone in the hallway, I collapse against the wall, gasping for air. Fear tangles with arousal inside me, and I know everything about my feelings are wrong. I can still feel his breath on my neck, the anticipation of his kiss burns across my body.

Of course, I know Knox enjoys seeing me this way, and I hate him, but then I go and practically orgasm at a single touch.

I'm so messed up, and now every inch of me is knotted up.

I march furiously back into the kitchen, pacing up and down the long room before I pour myself a glass of water. It shakes in my hand from my anger at him, at how much he turns me on.

Of course, he'd play with my head because I stupidly can't control my emotions around him.

Why had I thought anything else was possible with Knox?

CHAPTER FIVE

DRACON

As I walk along the corridor, the late-night hour begins to press against me, weighing me down. I know I should sleep—I exerted too much energy during our fight with the Spades and Aris, and I really should rest and catch up—but my adrenaline is still rushing through my veins, making my mind race. I've been trudging through the Tower's many floors since the rest of the gang retreated to their rooms after our meeting. It's been a couple of days now, and I still can't seem to quiet my thoughts.

I may have told Knox, Cassius, and Eve that we'd figure this out—with the Spades, with the vampires, with Aris—but what I didn't reveal to them was my worry. Especially when it comes to Aris.

Gangs are one thing. Humans, supernaturals, I've faced and beat them all, but a horseman of the apocalypse? That's a different animal. Cassius's spell wasn't strong enough to bind him, like it was supposed to. It hadn't even knocked the fucker out, only stunned him, and I know dark magic like that isn't something to take lightly. It only proves Aris's power. And the danger we're all in.

Especially Eve.

Part of me wonders why I'm even bothering with all this. Why do I care? If Eve is all Aris wants, then, shit, shouldn't I just pass her over and wipe my hands of her all together? Make one less problem for myself? The short answer is yes, I should.

The woman has no attachment to us. Not really. It would be easy to kick her into the fire, or easier yet, kill her myself.

But I can't.

Why?

One, if she's truly Aris's offspring, then that would mean she holds tremendous power. Power *we* could use.

We've been scrambling to hold onto our reign of this city since Saxon died, and the other gangs know that. They've been trying to claw us from the top while we've been weakened. Eve could be the addition we need to secure our spot again. No one would dare mess with us.

The second reason is more about my pride. Giving Eve up is a form of giving up, isn't it? Submitting. Admitting defeat. And the beast inside me refuses to do that.

I'm sure there are more reasons in there, but these two are the ones I'm the most focused on, the ones I'm refusing for. So, keeping Eve means I need to become an expert on Knox and his celestial *family* pretty fucking fast to save all our asses.

As I reach the tenth floor and continue my aimless

wandering, the sound of hurried whispers followed by whistling comes from one of the rooms at the far end of the hall. This level of the Tower has been dedicated solely to security. It's where some of our men camp out on late nights, as well as where our vaults and weapons are stored. Ex-military, supernaturals, people with special skills—we've hired them all if they're valuable to us. And tonight, from the noise and lights flashing from the surveillance room, I bet they're taking advantage of the late hour and their lack of supervision and goofing off. Something that's inexcusable and I'm going to rectify right now.

Temper flaring, I march down the hall to where the flashing lights and hurried whispers are coming from. It enrages me to think they're ignoring their responsibilities, especially with the enemies we have in Andover alone. What are we paying them for if they're just going to spend their time fucking around?

The moment I step into the doorway, I'm confronted with a wall of flat screens, ones that are supposed to show the feeds of every security camera in the Tower and surrounding streets. Instead, I'm staring at the same image repeated on every one.

The main focus is the bed and the beautiful, curvaceous woman laying there with her hand between her legs.

I freeze on the spot, instantly recognizing the video they're watching. It's when Eve wanted to get revenge on me for bringing her so close to the edge when we'd first met. She'd decided to finish herself off, bring herself to orgasm, despite the camera.

And the way she stared into the camera...it was almost as if she'd wants me to watch. Which I do. Transfixed by the way she strokes her own pussy and groped her breasts, quickly giving herself the relief I'd cruelly denied her.

She'd hoped it'd been my punishment then, when really, it only had made me more entranced by her.

"Dude, dude! Play it again!" the one guard barks, shoving his friend who's sitting in the chair beside him.

Blinding fury pushes against my control, my inner beast wanting to protect its newest plaything—its claim —at all cost. It doesn't like other men ogling over what it's deemed as his.

And mine.

"Sweet Jesus, look at her." The guard leans in and licks his lips. "Is there a way we can turn on the volume on this thing?"

"Are you out of your fucking mind? I don't need someone hearing anything." The other man is rubbing himself outside his pants, the fabric stretching tight over his obvious erection. "We're dead if someone finds out what we're doing in here."

"Why? She's just some whore," the first replies. "Clearly they're keeping her around for a little action."

Right then, Eve arches her back, her head pressing into the pillow as her body quivers from her building orgasm, and the guard leans in closer to the screen, practically salivating.

"Oooh, yeah. That's it, baby." He hits his friend in the arm. "Do you think the Kings will let me have a whack at her when they're done? After they toss her out?"

My feet carry me into the room without my permission. One second, I'm standing in the doorway, listening to this asswipe talk about Eve, my anger blazing, and the next I have him by the throat, lifting him off the floor. I don't think I've ever been so furious in my entire life, and I've lived a long fucking time. My entire body is shaking, my inner monster loving the way the man's face is turning bluer by the second. But it's too impatient to allow him a slow death, so a quick squeeze and twist of the wrist, and his neck snaps. Every limb goes dead, and I toss him onto the floor like the garbage he is.

Blood rushes behind my ears, drowning out all other sounds. But when I whirl around, I find the other guard has toppled over his chair in a desperate attempt to get away, his mouth open in a permanent scream.

I grab the first thing closest to me. A keyboard. Grip it tight and swing.

Keys fly. As do teeth and blood. But I'm not satisfied. I continue to pummel him until the keyboard has snapped almost in half and the side of his face is caved in, his body slumped on the floor.

If he's not dead yet, he will be soon. Especially based on the pool of blood growing rapidly under him by the second.

Throwing whatever's left of the scrap onto the carcass, I turn back to the screens. Twenty-four of them stare back at me, all with the frozen picture of Eve mid-orgasm, head thrown back, back arched and mouth opened.

She's enjoying every second of her revenge.

And little did she know, so am I.

Watching her writhe on the bed, coupled with the adrenaline of the fresh kills still pumping through my veins, has my cock rock hard. Remembering exactly how tight that pussy felt wrapped around my dick, those thick thighs squeezing me as we flew stories high in my partly shifted form.

Fucking her was everything I thought it would be and more, but what had really surprised me was the time after. When I was knotted inside her and we lay beside the pool, simply...talking. It was oddly intimate. More personal than sex had ever been for me before. Any women I'd been with had been a quick fuck-and-dump. Onto the next. My inner predator never connected to any of them, just saw them as a way to scratch a temporary itch. But with Eve—I don't know. It felt different.

I'm wondering if it has to do with the power she possesses. As a creature of great magic and power myself, I can recognize the benefits of having a person like that close. Maybe even make them mate material.

I shake my head to clear it. What the fuck am I thinking here? Mate? Absolutely fucking not. I don't have time for that shit. With our enemies, caring about anyone automatically puts a target on their back. They can be used against me as leverage. As a clear weakness to exploit.

Like Saxon.

I can't afford that right now.

We can't afford that right now.

The sound of hurried footsteps at the far end of the

hall has my ears pricking up. By their long, confident strides, I know it's Cassius before he pops his blond head into the surveillance room. And when he does, his gaze swings from me, to the dead men on the floor, to the screens covered in the paused image of Eve.

"Whatcha up to?" he says in a sing-song way. His deep blue irises darken to almost black, which is normally the first step before he loses control of his demon completely.

Despite the change in him, he flicks his hair out of his face and sucks in a sharp breath through the nose, like he's already taken some of the drugs he uses to leash the monster inside him. Only this time, it doesn't seem like he took enough.

"Cassius…" I growl a warning.

He rubs his nose excessively, turning the skin red. "I know," he snaps, as if he knows exactly what I'm about to say. "Knox depleted my stash, so I'm handling it."

Cassius has only gone full evil on us once—when he'd first joined me and Saxon as the Kings—and that was enough to prove to us that we needed him in our corner. He was an uncontrollable killing machine. Rage unlike I've ever seen before had him slaughtering any poor soul that got close enough. Man, woman, and yes, even children. It didn't matter. He was blinded by the chaos and the need to destroy. So, when he'd discovered that cocaine helped feed and settle the demon, I didn't discourage his newly formed drug habit.

But if it ever stopped working, well, I would be faced with a hard decision.

I'd more than likely have to take him out.

Like he's a fucking wet dog or something, Cassius shakes out his entire body, and when he looks at me again, he paints on an overstretched smile.

"So," he begins again, "getting another peek of our little Miss Eve?"

"Not me," I reply and step over the one dead security guard to stand before him.

"Ah. I see. Jerking on the job."

My hackles bristle as the memory of what I'd walked into surges forward again. My inner animal didn't want anyone to look at her that way.

I didn't want anyone to look at her that way.

Staring at the blood, Cassius tsks, pretending to be disappointed. "It's so hard to find good help these days, isn't it?"

"Why are you here, besides to annoy the shit out of me?" I bite out through a clenched jaw.

"I'm here to be the bearer of more bad news," he says.

Fuck. Great.

My entire body tenses. "What the fuck do you mean?"

"Remember the two containers that were hit during our last delivery? The one I fucking took personally?"

Of course, I did. We'd lost a lot of money on that deal because of it.

"It happened again. While we were facing off with the Spades and Knox's Ghostrider-wannabe brother."

"What?"

"Our containers in Pablo's yard. Five of them this time. Cleaned out."

Rage consumes me, fire licking my insides. The electric charge of the shift ripples over my skin, and I can feel the beast pushing against my human, wanting dominance. Even Cassius steps back.

"There's something else," he says, reaching into the pocket of his leather jacket. He pulls out a small USB flash drive and walks over to the computer desk. Kicking the dead man out of his way, he plugs it into the side of the main screen, presses a few things with the mouse, and waits until every image of Eve is replaced by the grainy black-and-white one of a storage container yard by the harbor. He steps aside to give me a better view.

"What's this?" I ask automatically.

"Pablo's. Watch."

Begrudgingly, I lean forward and focus on the blurry picture, seeing stacked metal boxes, a chain-link fence, and the back of an unmarked box truck. Cassius clicks the mouse a few times to speed up the recording, and once a few shadowy figures appear at the corner of the screen, he hits play.

Right there are the fucking rats, arms full of our guns and ammunition, heading for the truck to load *our* shit. *Steal* our money.

It's all captured on video. But who is it?

Peering at the screen, I try to make out faces or anything recognizable. Since it's night and the quality of the cameras at Pablo's place is shit, my sharpened eyesight is struggling to focus on the blurry shapes.

"Keep watching," Cassius encourages then points to the center of the screen. "Here."

Annoyance growing, I wait as the six or so men go back and forth, loading our weapons into the car. With each pass, my anger grows. Whoever these fuckers are, they're going to pay.

Finally, the men climb into the back of the truck and the doors slam shut, but before they pull off, another man comes out from behind the containers. Tall, wide, and wearing a striped jumpsuit and ginny tee. Even through the terrible video, the many chains around his next glisten. It gives his identity away immediately.

Dimitri. The Russian dark fae prince, a dickhole who's had it out for Cassius, and us by association, for years.

His gaze finds the camera, staring straight at us like he can see us watching him behind the computer, and he points. Then, the fucker throws his head back and laughs manically.

I throw my fist into the screen, shattering the glass and setting off a chain reaction for the others to shut down. As I straighten, my reflection stares back at me— dark strands of hair out of place, predator-yellow eyes glowing, and smoke spilling from my nostrils and lips. My knuckles are bleeding, my skin sliced up, but I don't feel any pain. Only blinding, raw fury.

Dimitri's goal had been to mock us. He'd wanted us to know that it was him and his gang of shitheads who took our money. That he isn't afraid of the Kings of Eden anymore because we've grown weak.

That was his fatal mistake.

Now, they're all going to die.

CHAPTER SIX

EVE

It's late at night. Or, I should say, it's ungodly early morning, but for some reason, I'm woken up by thundering footsteps and angry whispers coming down the hallway toward my door. I want to ignore them—I know I should—but when I recognize both Cassius and Dracon's voices saying words like "…kill them" and "…no mercy," I sit up in bed, too curious about who they're threatening this time. Aris? The Spades? Cobra Strike? They have too many enemies to keep track of.

And I guess I do, too.

That thought has me ripping off the covers and pushing out of bed.

"Have you thought anymore about Eve?" Cassius asks in a low tone, and the mention of my name in the mix of deadly words has my stomach clenching. The shadows moving underneath the doorframe tell me they are passing by my room. Their footsteps begin to fade as they continue down the hall.

"I know what you said the other night, but I've known you long enough to know that what you say and what you think are usually two different things," he goes on.

"I don't know what you're talking about," Dracon's gruff voice replies.

"You can't tell me you're not at least a little concerned about her powers and what Knox said about five horsemen. Killing her off would be the easiest solution."

Shit.

"She can also be useful to us…" His words become too hushed to make out as they enter the next room.

Useful? What does that mean?

I wait a few more seconds before opening my door and poking my head through. As expected, when I peer into the corridor, I find it empty, Cassius's and Dracon's mumbles continuing from a nearby room. The living room, if I were to guess.

With one last glance at my empty bed, I creep out of my bedroom on light feet and head toward the mumbles. I hear one of the men's shoes clicking against the hardwood floors and follow them through the foyer, making sure to stay far enough behind to not be spotted.

"You and I both know Knox has a special set of skills—ones we've never seen before. It's because of what he is," Dracon explains. As I turn the corner, I spot the back of Cassius's blond hair as he strides into the living room. I quickly press my back against the wall behind an expensive looking vase with long, spindly looking leaves coming out of it. There's no way I'm getting any closer.

Dracon keeps going. "If we add Eve to our ranks, she can help us solidify our place at the top of the food chain again."

"You want to…weaponize her?" Cassius sounds a bit surprised. And a little ticked.

"I want the Kings to be number-one again," he responds simply. "Before Saxon died, no one would have *dared* go against us. Or challenge us. Now, it's starting to feel like we cut off one monster's head and five more sprout up."

Wait… Did he just say Saxon died? I've been wondering who the guy was considering I've heard his name brought up previously and barely received any information on him.

"That's an over exaggeration," Cassius quips in annoyance, but Dracon bites back with even more force.

"Is it? We have every gang up our asses from all over the East Coast. And now from across the fucking world."

"It's nothing we can't handle though," Cassius says, drawing me back to the conversation at hand. "It's always been us against the world. What makes this any different?

"Everything."

My heart beats faster. The real reason Dracon is keeping me alive isn't because he cares for me at all. That's a childish fantasy—one I better snap myself out of ridiculously fast. He wants to *use me*. And not in the sexual way, like I want him to. In a "I'm making her into a machine" kind of way.

"She's so young," Cassius protests, and my chest warms at his empathy. Knowing Cassius, it's coming from a heartless place, but at least I get some sympathy points. "She's brand new to this—all of this. Our world—"

"It doesn't matter."

I know Dracon is known to have a heart of stone. But shit…what an asshole!

"Keeping her alive and in our sight helps us," he states, emphasizing every word, "that's it."

"If anything, we could always just keep her around as a fun piece of ass," Cassius says sarcastically, followed by a quick laugh. It is clearly a joke. It still makes anger stir inside me.

The demon is just as bad. I wasn't delusional enough to think these maniacs cared about me—Cassius did carve his name into my hip for fuck's sake—but to hear him say I'm just something to fuck whenever he wants makes fury whirl within me. I'm not an object. I'm not *theirs*. If it wasn't for the psycho fire-breathing horseman trying to kidnap me, I wouldn't even need to be here with them. I'd handle Franco and the Spades on my own. I'd done it before; I could do it again.

In my musings, I hadn't realized when the conversation I'd been eavesdropping on went silent, and my heartbeat speeds up. A hand snaps out, seizing me behind the neck and yanks me out of my hiding spot behind the vase.

Oh shit!

I lock gazes with Dracon, his yellow eyes catching the light and seeming to glow. His nostrils flare, drawing in my scent, and I wonder briefly if dragons have a heightened sense of smell too, like other shifters.

Apparently so, because as he inhales his muscles turn to stone, like he can sense something on me that I can't.

And it's doing things to him.

Slowly, his chin dips. "You're prime," he growls, which makes me blanche.

"Ex-Excuse me?" My entire body trembles under his weighted gaze.

"You're in heat," he replies.

Like a cat or something?

I probably should be disgusted by such a comment, but my heartbeat only speeds up. Dracon uses his grip on me to pull me fully into the living room, fully presenting me to Cassius, who's grin is as wide as the Cheshire Cat.

Not sure what else to do, I embed my nails into his arm, hoping it'll be enough for him to release me, but like always, he seems unfazed by the pain.

Cassius looks at me hungrily, making my skin prickle all over.

"Can you fucking let me go?" I bite out as I try everything to remove his hold from the back of my neck.

"Why should I, when I can tell from the scent of your arousal that you're enjoying it?" Dracon answers.

Heat curls in my lower belly, but I keep the truth I'm

hiding off my face. "I don't know what you're talking about."

"I'm an Apex predator, Eve. My nose *never* lies."

Was that a joke? Or was that what Dracon's kind was actually called? I've seen him transform into multiple creatures with my own eyes, when a normal shifter can only take the form of one. Whatever he is, it must be really rare.

He turns to Cassius. "She likes being handled rough."

"Oh, she sure does," he says. "Just ask her about our little fuck-session on Dimitri's car."

Immediately, Dracon releases me and his massive frame spins Cassius's way. "What did you just say?" He growls every word, as if this news both surprises and enrages him. Pulling his shoulders back, he instantly looks bigger. More menacing.

Even Cassius notices and shifts back a step. His gaze flicks to me and confusion flashes over his face.

Dracon moves closer to him, muscles strained with tension. Then he whirls around, focusing all that anger and intimidation onto me. "You fucked him?"

His blunt words make me wince. My mouth opens to reply, but I don't know what to say. His fury and the question have rendered me unable to form a coherent thought.

His impatience has him spinning back to Cassius. "When did this happen? When did you fuck her?"

"Shit, Drac, what does it matter? Why do you fucking care so much?"

"Answer me!" His voice booms and bounces all over the massive room.

"The night of the auction, Drac! Fuck!" Cassius's form begins to blur, his face contorting before our eyes as his demon rears up. It doesn't seem to like being challenged, even from a supposed friend or partner.

"Why do you fucking care?" I personally don't understand where this rage is coming from, but it's starting to trigger my own. Does he think he owns my body or something? That I have no say in who I sleep with?

Cassius hadn't really played fair that night when he'd chased me down, trapped me, and fucked me, but I doubt Dracon would care about any of that. He seems to just be mad that he wasn't the only one who'd indulged in carnal sin with me.

He's jealous.

I've seen him mad before, but this is something else.

A jealous Dracon is a deadly Dracon.

"Did he cum in you?" he barks next.

He didn't just ask that...

"Are you out of your mind?" I shout back. I'm not going to answer that.

In a flash, he closes the space between us and his fingers tangle in my hair. He rips my head back and pain shoots across my skull. Tears gather in my eyes and I cry out.

"Let go of me, you psycho!"

Dracon leans in close. So close, his warm breath brushes across my cheek and ear when he speaks, this time growling each word. "Did. He. Cum. Inside. You. Eve?"

I can barely answer. The stabbing pain in my head is all I can focus on.

Swallowing hard, I'm able to rasp out, "Fuck...no..."

A bead of sweat rolls down my temple, and his lips touch my skin to catch it. "What was that, Eve? I couldn't hear you."

"I said fuck no! He jizzed all over the inside of the car! Now get off me!"

I can't even believe I'm saying this out loud. It's ridiculous.

With one last jerk of my hair, he sends me to my knees in the middle of the floor. Then he laughs. Loud and manically.

He's absolutely lost it. Insane.

Cassius freezes, his form still fuzzy around the edges, as if even the demon within is unsure what's going on.

We both stay still and silent as Dracon laughs, me trying to relieve the new pounding in my head and Cassius poised and trying to gauge Dracon's next move.

It takes a few tense moments, but Dracon finally stops his maddening laughter. And when he does, he directs his next words to Cassius. "If you didn't cum inside her, it doesn't count."

"What the fuck, Drac?" he snaps back.

His expression smooths over, becoming the permanent silent scowl I've grown used to. "I was the first to fuck her then. Whatever you two did didn't mean anything. I was first."

Chest heaving, I glare up at him with narrowed eyes. "Does that really mean so much to you?"

When his gaze falls upon me again, his head tilts to the side, reminding me of an animal studying its prey. His eyes grow intense, sliding up and down my body.

My heart skips, and I burn up under his stare because there's something more behind them. I feel my cheeks heating up and when he closes the distance between us, I step back.

"You have no idea how beautiful you are, or what you do to us, do you?" Dracon pauses only when my heels hit the wall and I'm pinned beneath him.

From the corner of my eye, Cassius shifts closer, studying me just as carefully. Is he waiting to see what Dracon will do? Is this just a big game to them?

I blink, looking up at him, saying, "Feelings mutual. You irritate me almost daily." I grin.

He doesn't react to my words, but a half smile curls on his lips. "I love it when you get snarky. It makes it so much more fun." He reaches over and strokes the back of his knuckles down my cheek.

I push him away. "Don't pretend, Dracon. I heard what you said about me. I'm not just an instrument for you to use."

"Do you want *more*?" He arches an eyebrow, seeming somewhat taken aback by my question.

"I didn't think monsters were capable of love."

His tongue slides across his lower lip, staring at me, something shifting behind his gaze.

"If you're searching for love, Eve, you're in the wrong place. There's no such thing as forever and soul mates. But what I can offer you is something you desire. Something that I see in your eyes, that I smell on your scent. And make no mistake, I will keep you as mine. Maybe that will be enough for you?"

His response makes me slightly nauseated. "I-I didn't say I wanted your love." It's not something I've ever admittedly wanted, not after growing up in a loveless family with Mom. My life has been fated to be a chaotic mess from the beginning, considering who my father is. But now, I find myself caught in this monster's web, and I hate myself for being attracted to him. For wanting him to just shut the hell up and kiss me.

He laughs. "What do you want then, Eve?"

I swallow hard and glance over to Cassius, who simply watches us with interest. "I don't know," I admit truthfully.

"Good girl," he says, cupping the sides of my face. "You're finally being honest."

I grind my teeth, but when he steps even closer to me, I tense up. His breath washes across my cheek and ear, where he whispers, "Now, shall we do something about your other need?"

He's suddenly pressing up against me, his thick cock nestled against my stomach, and I know instantly what he's talking about.

"I don't think—" His mouth grazes mine, stealing my words and breath. He kisses me with passion, with fire, with dominance. My pulse races, and despite having my hands pressed flush to his chest, I don't push him away.

Something must be broken inside me, but things are a lot more complicated now between the Kings and I. My guard remains up.

Thing is, I've never had anyone look out for me so

possessively before. Call me crazy, but I like feeling wanted.

Sure, I still need to deal with the crap they were talking about as I eavesdropped, but Dracon isn't the only one who knows how to get his way.

And with the way he kisses, he ignites arousal deep in my gut. I can't get him out of my mind, and how much I'd love to wrap myself around his body.

Our bodies are flush, and I kiss him back. I curl my fingers around the collar of his shirt, holding on. The way he tastes is pure addiction, so who says I can't have fun while playing in the den of monsters?

After all, as a daughter of the horseman of apocalypse, how much less monstrous am I?

The groan in his throat only turns me on further as his tongue pushes past my lips and tangles with mine.

His scent consumes me—musk, sex, and something earthy. It's ridiculous how much smell alone can drive me crazy.

"Want me to stop?" he whispers against my mouth as his hand falls to my breast and pinches my nipple between his fingers. I'm only wearing a tee with nothing underneath and he's taking advantage of that.

"Don't you dare stop," I growl, coaxing a devilish grin from the man.

He's painfully handsome, rendering me useless. Everything about him is perfect, the regal way he holds himself, the dominating voice, the possessive way he holds me. But beneath it all is an animal who is capable of tearing me apart.

"Good to hear." He's suddenly got me into his strong

arms and off my feet. I loop my legs around his hips, my arms wrapping around the back of his neck.

I notice Cassius doesn't say a word, though he's watching us intently.

Dracon grinds his groin against the heat between my legs, reminding me of what he promises. "What should I do with you to teach you a lesson?"

"Mmm," I moan. "Sounds like you've got a conundrum." He props me against the back of the couch, and I lower my feet to the floor. His mouth finds mine again, hands ripping my clothes off with ease, the sharpness of the claws pushing out of his fingertips shredding my pajamas. Pieces of fabric fall around my feet, and a chill curls around me as I end up naked in front of two Alphas.

There's a groan from Dracon's throat, his gaze sliding down my body. His brow suddenly furrows and he snatches my arm, forcing me to turn sideways.

"Hey, not so rough," I mutter.

But the moment I see what he's inspecting on my hip, his thumb running over the words "Cassius" cut into my skin like he's trying to rub it off, I understand.

"You carved your fucking name into her hip?" he snaps, jerking his attention to Cassius, who's grinning.

"Someone had to lay claim over her should we ever misplace her." He laughs at his own joke, while Dracon looks ready to rip off his head.

"It's a dick move," I say. "But payback will be amazing."

"I look forward to it, baby girl." He blows me a kiss.

"I regret nothing and, if you want to Drac, go ahead and leave your own mark on her cute ass."

"No," I blurt. "I'll get a say in it next time."

Dracon roars, holding me possessively, snarling at Cassius. "For that, you can fucking watch."

Oh, his vindictive streak does surprise me. Nonetheless, there's a thrill having someone like Dracon go all caveman over me.

Turning on me, there's no hesitation in the way he lifts me to perch on the back of the couch and pushes himself between my legs, forcing them open.

"I'm going to fuck you now." There's darkness in his eyes, and I struggle to breathe from how hard he holds me.

But I'm not one to steer away from pain. If I've learned anything since moving in with these Kings, it's that it gets me off.

So, I tug at his belt and push his pants over his hips. His cock jerks out almost like a Jack-in-the-box, and I love how they do that. I wrap my hand around his massive offering, loving how silky and yet so hard it feels.

"You're killing me from the sidelines," Cassius grits out, and I look at him, the words on my lips stolen when Dracon's hand falls between my thighs. His fingers glide over my pussy, pushing open my lips. His touch grazes my clit, and I moan at how tightly I'm wound up, how turned on I am.

"Fuck you," Dracon growls over to Cassius.

When he pushes two fingers into me, I tense and

arch my body. Cassius already has his cock out, palming his heavy flesh.

I'm not quite sure if they are going to break out into a fight or start a tug of war with me in the middle of them.

"Good girl," Dracon tells me, distracting me, while I tighten my hold on his cock. My body lurches back the faster he fingers me. Without warning, he withdraws his sticky fingers, completely aware of the effect he has on me based on the smile curling on his lips.

He barely gives me time to complain as he's pushing my legs wider, the tip of his cock already pressing into me.

Looming over me, his face is a mask of pure elation. I try to speak but it comes out as a garbled gasp as he pushes in deeper, one inch at a time, holding my stare the whole time.

"Wrap those sexy legs around me," he commands, which I obey, gasping for air from how much I need this.

Powerful hands grasp onto my ass, and suddenly he lifts me toward him as he spears deeply into me. I cry out with the beautiful pain he causes, and I groan for more. I dig my fingers into his round shoulders, holding on, and he surges in and out of me.

Desire and submission are tangled in the strange relationship I have with Dracon, and yet I desire more.

"Are you okay?" he asks me, slowing down, making me even more aware of just how full he makes me. His cock is thick, and I feel every inch of him, holding me stretched open.

He's glancing over to Cassius then back at me.

I look over at my demon lover, and something stings in my chest to see him watching with lust in his gaze. Despite all his crazy, he's grown on me, and well, I have a fantasy I'd love to explore.

"I want Cassius to join us," I state breathily.

"No," Dracon snaps.

"Then this ends now," I rebut, pushing against his chest, giving back just as much. "Please, Dracon. I've always wanted to know what it's like to be fucked by two men. Will you take that away from me?"

When he just stares at me looking ready to explode, I stretch out my hand to Cassius, calling him to me with a curl of my finger.

To my surprise, Dracon doesn't attack Cassius, but stares at him with daggers in his eyes. I'm not quite sure if that's a challenge or what, but Cassius has a huge, satisfied grin.

"Fuck you, Cassius. And fine. You either come join us or fuck off out of here. And next time you think of signing your name on something that belongs to me, I'll rip your throat out."

Cassius doesn't need to be told twice, because in moments, his cock is pressing up against my ass, not paying heed to Dracon's threat. Part of me wonders if you can even kill a demon.

"Didn't want to cramp your style," he mocks, and his cockiness makes me giggle.

Dracon groans from me squeezing his cock. All while Cassius's fingers are running across my ass crack and purrs in my ear, "Oh, I see you are already so wet for me." Pushing a finger into me, a thrill runs through me, the nerves on my clit tingling.

"Are you ready?" Dracon mutters, his voice darkening when he lifts his gaze to Cassius.

"I was ready before you."

Dracon growls.

"Please," I manage as Cassius slides his cock into my ass. I hold onto Dracon as he moves one hand to my breast, kneading it, pinching my nipple.

I arch against him, and Cassius works his way deeper into me, taking his time, which I appreciate. "It hurts a bit but also feels so incredible." My hips start to rock as the sensation of having him deeply inside me has me panting.

"I know," Cassius says. "But you'll find out how good it feels to have us both."

I'm pinned between these two powerful Kings. They begin moving, finding their rhythm easily, sliding in and out of me. Slowly at first, and I'm writhing, moaning at the delicious friction they ignite. Dracon never pauses on pinching my nipple, then moves to the other, driving me insane with need.

There's no pause to get used to just how big these Alphas are, or that they are now moving faster in and out of me. Fucking me, pushing me to a point of pleasure and pain. That's when I discover the perfect way to rub my clit against Dracon's dick.

I moan louder, staring at the intensity in Dracon's eyes, the pleasure consuming him as he strokes everything inside me. "Oh, god."

They drive into me harder now, seeming to stare at

each other as if competing on who can go faster. And here I thought we were flying fast before. I clutch onto Dracon, holding on, Cassius gripping my hips, guiding them as they both thrust into me.

"I'm down here," I have to remind them. "Or do you two prefer to eye fuck each other instead?"

Dracon looks down at me, apology in his eyes, while Cassius has his lips on my neck. "Sorry," he whispers.

"You're right. I'm possessive as fuck over you, and I'm letting that ruin it. Forgive me," Dracon states.

"You got it," I say, and the moment we fall back into a groove that leaves me covered in goosebumps, I moan, joining in with my own gyrating moves.

My throat grows hoarse from my cries of pleasure, and selfishly let them take what they want from me.

Their hips jerk violently into me, thrusting upward, making me dizzy.

"Is this what you want?" Dracon growls.

"Yes. God yes," I sing out, wishing to hold onto the buzzing sensation building inside me, loving the wild fantasies that these men satisfy.

With it, my body responds by shuddering. I convulse, screaming out my climax that grips me at the very foundation. I can barely breathe, the orgasm breaking me, spreading through me like wildfire.

My thighs tremble around Dracon's hips as I tremble.

The men snarl, their bodies tensing. "Fuck," Cassius cries out.

"That's it, milk my cock," Dracon growls.

They're making low-throaty sounds, and I feel the

hot explosion of cum bursting inside me. Rammed all the way in, they have me trapped between their bodies. Spurts of cum fill me, I feel its warmth, and they're still going. With it comes the heavy thickness from Dracon's cock. He's swelling, knotting in me.

A flare of panic fills me that I've completely run out of room with Cassius still inside me.

But they don't seem bothered. Their hands roam over my body, relentlessly spilling their seed in me, so much that I feel it dripping down the inside of my thighs.

We remain locked together. Me floating on a high, the men's growls so animalistic, I fear I've lost them to their darker sides.

Breaths racing, Dracon finally meets my gaze and Cassius kisses my neck. I sense him drawing out of my ass, and I miss him already.

"You are spectacular," Cassius gasps and collapses over the back of the couch and onto his back. He smiles happily, while Dracon peppers my face with kisses.

"Let's take a shower," he tells me. "It will help clean us up and then I'll take you to your room to rest."

"I'd like that," I reply, my head lolling against his chest as exhaustion washes over me.

With my legs still wrapped around his middle and Dracon's dick locked inside me, he walks us through the house. I try to remember what we were talking about before I ended up having sex with two Kings.

But I'm too tired to think, let alone sort out the emotions swirling inside me at this moment. I may have to save that for another time.

"Eve," Dracon whispers, waking me up. Just in the few seconds it's taken to cross the Tower, I've drifted off, pleasantly comfortable in his arms with him still knotted inside me.

I guess a girl could get used to this.

When I lift my head and look around, I realize we're entering Dracon's trophy room, ironically the first place we'd met and where he keeps his priceless and magical collectibles. I had expected him to take us to my room, not his, and I'm not quite sure what his motives are for bringing me here.

Instantly, I feel vulnerable. Even though he's the one carrying me inside his most personal space, it still feels like I don't belong, like I'm sneaking inside.

He doesn't seem to notice my discomfort and heads straight for the bathroom. "No matter how pissed you are at me, or what you think we're planning, I have claimed you as mine. As ours. I'll give you everything you want, even what you don't know you need yet, but you will be mine."

I almost laugh at his admission, but a crazy part of me doesn't want to fight. I want to hold onto the idea that these men want me for *me*, that maybe for once I won't be all alone in this world.

So, I only nod and shut down my thoughts. This possessive King carries me into the massive standing shower and turns on the hot water. Everything is dark tiles and glass in here, with enough room for Cassius and Knox to join us if they wanted to. The idea has my core buzzing again.

When the ten different jets begin to spray us with pressurized warm water, Dracon moves us to the seating bench so that I can sit on his lap in our connected position. He picks up a loofa from a nearby rack and bar of soap and starts lathering it up.

I rest my head in the curve of his neck, my eyes already drifting closed.

I don't know the exact moment the change happened between us, but I want to believe Dracon wants to protect me. I can't take on Aris and Franco alone.

The Kings of Eden are my best chance of survival. But I'm losing myself to them, too, and I don't know what scares me more.

As Dracon sweeps the soapy loofa over my back and down my arms, he begins to hum a song I don't recognize. He seems lost in his thoughts, and I wonder if he even knows he's doing it. As his throat vibrates against my cheek with his sorrowful tune, I'm reminded how much I still don't know about this man. About any of these men, really.

"Um, Dracon?" I start, my tone low.

"Hm?" He continues to rub my skin in small circles.

"How old are you?"

His hand pauses. "Why are you asking?"

"Because I want to know." I pull back so that I can look at him fully. "I know nothing about you."

"Yes, you do," he counters.

"No, I don't. Not really."

His brow creases in confusion. "You know more than most people do."

I believe that. The only thing Dracon seems to want to be known for his deadly reputation. He prefers the rest to be a secret.

But I want to know more. Especially if I'm going to be living with the man. And sleeping with him.

Dracon sighs heavily and his gaze searches my face. "You really want to know my age? It matters that much to you?"

I nod. "It's just another piece of you I'm trying to learn."

"Would you believe me if I said I lost count?" he says with a flicker of a smile.

I chuckle. "You're an old man, huh?"

He shrugs. "Not nearly as old as Knox, but yes, I'm up there."

That is extremely vague. I decide to switch gears.

"Was that song you were humming before?" I ask.

His eyes widening tells me he hadn't realized he'd

been mumbling it. After a few beats of silence, he answers, "It was a song from my pack. In Scandinavia."

"Scandinavia?" Had I heard him right?

"Just over a thousand years, maybe, if I were to guess."

I shove my hands against his chest in disbelief. "You're fucking with me."

"You said you wanted to know."

I did—I do. But, shit, he's old.

These Kings are out of my league on so many levels. But now that I have him opening up—at least a little—I want to ask the one question that's been plaguing me for a while.

"Dracon…"

He eyes me cautiously. "Yes?"

"Who was Saxon?"

His entire body tenses, his muscles rigid against me, and I regret bringing up the name at all. He says nothing for a long moment, and I watch as a range of different emotions pass over his face. Anger, sorrow, regret, grief —I'm not sure which one he's about to unleash on me, but when his gaze drops to the floor and his shoulders drop, my heart tugs in sympathy. Whoever Saxon was, he was close to him, and if what I'd overheard before is true, he's also dead.

I quickly try to recover. "I'm sorry. You don't need to tell me if—"

"No," he cuts me off. "It's okay."

I bit my lower lip sheepishly, wishing I'd kept my mouth shut and just dropped the entire thing.

Dracon sets down the soap and loofa and pushes a

strand of wet hair behind my ear before going on. "Saxon is—*was*—my friend. Fuck, you could say I considered him family, if my own blood didn't despise me like they did. He was the closest person to me, the only one I had that I trusted and respected even more than myself. It was his idea to form the Kings of Eden. His idea to recruit Dracon and Knox and take over the city. He…" Dracon swallows with great difficulty. "He was the best of all of us."

"And you lost him?" I ask gently, afraid to push too much and have him shut down on me.

"I fucking murdered him."

I blink, his harsh words and tone taking me off guard. "You didn't—you couldn't have."

"I might as well," he replies, the anger and coldness sliding back over his expression. "It was my mistake that cost him his life. My stupidity. He trusted me and I let him down."

"I don't believe that," I say. It just doesn't make sense. "It's true."

It's clear Saxon's death is a heavy burden Dracon's been carrying on his shoulders. His guilt's been crushing him, and even if the other men don't believe it's his fault Saxon's dead, Dracon is convinced it is. I'm not sure there's a soul alive that could make him believe otherwise.

Sorrow winds around me, and I press a palm to his cheek. His chin lifts to meet my eyes again. He's not used to such a soft and warm gesture, I can tell. But when he leans into my touch, I know it's doing its job to comfort him. That's all I really want to do right now.

"Can you tell me what happened?" I question, trying to ease him further.

"Aren't you afraid? I just told you I killed my best friend," he says.

"Yeah, but I know you've killed many, *many* other people. Hell, I've seen you tear apart the Black Spades when you're only half-shifted into a murderous beast creature. It isn't anything I don't know already."

He snorts.

"Look, you don't have to tell me shit. I know that. But I want to try and understand you three better. Especially if I'm going to be staying here for a while."

"I'll tell you this," he begins, considering his next words before continuing. "What happened to Saxon is my fault. That's not an over exaggeration. I may not have been the one to pull the trigger that ended his life, but because of me, because of *my* mistake, he died during a job. A routine hit. But I had been too arrogant, too careless back then. The Kings were on top, and I was floating on that high. I thought we were untouchable. So, when the fucking asshole came in after me to pull me out of the mess I'd made, what happened?"

"Oh, shit…" I mutter, my hand falling away..

"Exactly," he says. "His blood is on my hands. It's something I'll have to live with forever."

"Is that what he'd want for you though?" I ask. "It sounds like he wanted to protect you. Save you. He knew he was risking his life for a reason."

"But he shouldn't have had to. If I'd listened to him in the first place—"

"I don't know if—"

"You're right," he snaps, stealing the rest of my thought of me. "You don't know."

I clamp my mouth shut, knowing there's no way I'm going to win this argument. Not when Dracon's guilt runs so deep. This is something he has to work out for himself. Anything I say will only trigger his internal rage and self-loathing right now, and I don't want to do that, either.

"Okay," I say softly and shift in his lap. He's still knotted inside me, and it's forcing me to stay put through this hard conversation. If we weren't attached, I probably would've left the shower by now. "I'm sorry I asked."

He shakes his head. "No, no. It's not that."

"I get it. This is hard for you," I reply.

He pauses. "It is."

"We all have our things. Regrets. Ghosts that'll haunt us forever. Things that'll never heal." I've done my fair share of shit I wish I hadn't. Actually, I'm going to add getting Kat kidnapped on that list too. "I'm not going to try to fix it for you or anything because, well, I can't. I can't take your guilt away, but I can tell you you're not alone.

"I don't know much about this Saxon guy, but if he cared for you half as much as you cared about him, he wouldn't want you suffering."

A flicker of a smile captures his lips. "I suffer everyday living with those two nutjobs without him here as a buffer."

"I'm sure Cassius and Knox would say the same

about you," I say, lightening my tone. It works because he chuckles.

"A hundred percent." Dracon wraps his massive arms around me, caging me in, and draws me flush against him.

My head tucks back into his neck and he inhales deeply, drawing in my scent. It probably should creep me out—the whole smelling me thing—but shifters are different that way and when Dracon does it, it makes me shiver with desire. It's like he's staking his claim on me, or sating his obsession.

"I wish you could've met him," he whispers. The sudsy loofa is back drawing circles up and down my spine, washing away the heaviness of the conversation we just shared and leaving only us, more stripped down and raw.

"You think he would have liked me?" I ask.

"More than that. He would have loved what you've done to me."

CHAPTER EIGHT

I move rapidly down the stairs of the Tower fire exit in the middle of the night.

Silence follows me, yet I keep rushing down with an urgency I don't quite understand. But my heart beats faster, my adrenaline's pushing me to get out of the building. It pulls at me like an elastic band tired around my middle. I can't explain it, but I keep going like I have to be somewhere. Yet, I can't for the life of me remember where.

It's dark and I'm barefoot, the cement steps cold, but I barely feel them. My mind's a blur of urgency and my thighs are smarting. But none of that matters.

Before I know it, I'm pushing the exit door open and stumbling outside onto a side street. Part of me expects some kind of alarm to go off, but there's nothing. Not a blip.

Night smothers the street, and there are hardly any cars in sight. But the moment a warm breeze washes over me, a jolt races up my spine.

I blink, disoriented.

It's like I've just opened up my eyes for real and I'm suddenly standing on the sidewalk in the middle of the night in my pajama shorts and tee.

With my heart banging wildly in my chest, I stumble around and tug on the fire exit door behind me, wrenching at the cold handle. It's locked. What the hell? Have I started to sleepwalk?

When a shadow falls over me, I whirl around and gasp at the sight.

Stunning is the first thought that comes to mind as I stare at the beautiful woman I recognize instantly. With that thought, a terrifying panic flares over me.

I met her at the auction night the Kings took me to a couple of weeks back. This woman with flowing silvery hair, pointy ears, and sharp cheekbones had accompanied Dimitri, the Russian dark fae prince.

She's wearing a full body jumpsuit as black as the night. The zipper running from her navel to throat is open halfway down the chest, revealing a lot of cleavage.

Cassius had called the women by a strange name. Something with an R, and it's just not coming to mind. But what I do remember clearly is that they are the embodiment of young women who've drowned or been killed in water. Not to mention, Cassius admitted he had killed one of their sisters.

A shiver races down my spine, and instead of asking her what she is doing there, something else slips from my mouth. "You're a rusalka," I gasp, now remembering what Cassius had called them.

Her perfect mouth tilts into a smile. "Good little girl. You remember me."

Before I can respond, she breaks into humming a song—the most beautiful tune I've ever heard. It seems to swirl around me and into my thoughts, luring me into its hypotonic embrace.

One moment, I am on the sidewalk with a rusalka, the next I'm sitting in the back seat of a black limo, pinned between two of the women, both in black bodysuits.

My head spins and I'm hyperventilating, gasping for air. "What the fuck? Let me out."

A black window keeps us divided from the driver, and outside the window I can see we're rushing along a freeway, night swallowing the landscape.

If I was panicking before, now I'm about to scream. "You kidnapped me? What the hell for?" My attempt to sound less scared comes out more like a shaky groan. Then I remember crystal clear how Cassius and I had sex in Dimitri's car before he ejaculated all over his black leather seats. God, it was a lot of cum too. Shit! I knew that stunt would come back and bite me in the ass.

"Look, it's Cassius you want, not me. Go after him, and I promise I won't stand in your way."

One of the women giggles, then says something in Russian to her friend, who begins to laugh as well as they look me up and down. Okay, I'm already on the brink of losing my shit, but now on top of that, I'm starting to feel insecure.

I tug down on my pajama tee while sitting next to

dolled up goddesses. "What do you want from me?" I demand, trying to shake off the insecurity.

But instead of waiting for them to spin me some lie or continue laughing at me, I sense my own power building, surging through my veins. It's linked to my emotions, I realize that, and I'm furious at being lured out of the Tower so easily.

I swallow hard, my fingers curling right around the hem of my T-shirt as I try to still my tremble. After everything, a girl can only take so much.

I glance outside the window to determine where exactly we are on the freeway, when a jolt of lightning tears through me, ripping at my despairing emotions. I flinch, and one of the women frowns at me.

Electricity crackles inside me, the air ripe with its bitterness. Then it happens.

Wild power bursts out of me, the sudden explosive release powerful enough to leave me reeling. The whole car shakes violently. I'm talking about rocking side to side like we'd been tossed into a washing machine

One of the rusalka shouts, grabbing hold of the seat in front of us just as the windows start shaking.

A heartbeat later, they explode. It's the only way to explain it. Shards of glass burst outward from the car with an explosive boom.

We all scream at that stage, and out of instinct, I duck forward, covering my head. Some of the pebbles of glass are whipped back into the car at us.

I grip the seat beneath me, terrifying myself that I have so little control over my power. That I can cause such destruction in seconds.

"You fucking cow!" one of the women yells at me. "What did you do? Stop it now!"

The car swerves across the road, throwing me against one rusalka, while the other screams as she holds onto the door with a death grip.

Harsh screeches of the skidding tires pierce my ears as we spin out of control. Wind tears into the car and the stench of burned tires suffocates me.

Gritting my teeth, I hold onto the seat, pressed up against a rusalka who's shouting something at the driver while her friend is tossed to the floor at my feet where she lands with a thud.

The car spins wildly, my head is spinning, too. We move faster, sickness kissing the back of my throat.

The guttural crank of the engine suddenly gives out, yet we keep spinning.

We hit something with a heavy thump, and we're all thrown forward. I smack into the divider between us and the driver, my brow and nose taking the brunt. Warmth dribbles from my nose, and I taste a metallic tang on the back of my throat.

I don't move as I catch my breath. The two rusalka are groaning, this is my chance to escape.

Desperation has me scrambling across the seat and behind one woman, crumbled on the floor and bleeding from a gash across her temple.

I shove open the door and leap out of the car.

Faint streetlights reveal an empty freeway with only cement barriers on either side of the road. I take the chance and run back the way we came.

I sprint madly on bare feet down the road and pray

that any oncoming traffic sees me. Glancing over my shoulder reveals I'm not as quick as I think I am. Both the women are chasing after me, and they're fast. I might have yelped, well aware I can't outrun them.

So I do the next best thing. I stop abruptly and turn toward them, tapping into the fury still bubbling in my veins.

They both lunge at me as the road begins to shake beneath me. I scream just as they slam into me, taking me off my feet. A sharp pain stabs at my back where I'd landed on something. Shit, that hurts.

But they're all over me while I spot huge cracks snaking up the barrier walls flanking the freeway. I might have screamed right then, scaring myself at my own power, while shoving and kneeing the bitches grabbing me, scratching me.

No matter how much my heart clenches, it doesn't stop me from shoving my hands into one of the women's chest, dislodging her from where she was crouched on top of me.

With a final push, she rocks off me and rolls away at the same time as a segment of the partition falls away from the wall. It comes down so fast there's no time to respond, and it lands flat on the rusalka. Squishing her.

One second she's there, then she's not, her scream stolen. Only a pool of blood seeps out from beneath the slab of the broken wall.

Ouch.

The other woman's scream pierces the night.

I scramble backward, dragging myself across the ground away from her.

Up on my feet, I run for my life once more. My hands curl, fear seeping into me. My actions killed the rusalka so easily that it scares me. I'm not a killer.

Something harsh and cruel grabs me by the back of my neck and with it comes that soft tune again. The one that has me whimpering because I know exactly what it means. I fight it, gritting my teeth, focusing on anything but the song. Pleading for my power to unleash now.

Her grip is cruel, fingernails digging into my skin. I whimper, yet I'm lulled between the pain and the soft tune burning into my thoughts.

She might be singing beautifully, but her twisted face is filled with fury and retribution. And despite my jaw muscles tensing, I have no willpower to fight back... to escape...to draw on my power.

Just as suddenly as it started, her song flatlines and her fist rushes for my face. Only then do I notice she's gripping a knife and the hilt connects with the side of my head.

Pain blooms deep and I wince, my knees giving out as darkness feathers at the corners of my eyes.

The last words I hear are, "You fucking bitch. I will enjoy breaking you after you killed my sister."

CASSIUS

*E*ve never leaves my mind. I try, but she's already in my veins and it's slowly killing me not having her next to me every second of the day. I've told myself and others she's just a great fuck, an irresistible fuck. Yet lying to myself isn't working.

Not anymore. I've tasted the beauty, had her pussy squeeze my cock, heard her screams. Fuck, I'm itching to get back to her. And that's not like me. I don't do relationships or anything beyond a fun time of wham-bam now get the hell out of my face.

Instead, I'm edgy as fuck. Especially each time I think back to Dracon's caveman possessiveness with her, fucking her tight little cunt.

My balls tighten at the memory of me taking her on the car at the auction night. How she fought me, but in the end she gave in and became pliant. She spread those legs for my cock. They all do eventually. Yet, Eve is different isn't she? Her scent has gotten into my head and I smell it everywhere.

Even now. I growl, my hand already sliding down my body as I lay in bed, naked, imagining her sitting on my face. I know that my obsession is deepening and that her being with the Kings will ruin her. How could it not? Each of us are more fucked up than the next. And yet I can't resist. I don't care. I want to dive into the darkest pits with her.

I picture those beautiful curves, her bouncing tits, how addictive it is to lay between her beautiful thighs. She's not a pushover. She's held together by strength and the chaos in her past. I saw that pain in her eyes, and after discovering she's the daughter of a horseman, well, she's just as fucked up as the rest of us.

She's perfect for me. After all, broken things stay together.

I palm my cock and groan, arching my back, thinking of pushing my cock into her tight little crevice. How good it'll feel to stretch her as I thrust roughly into her. Every inch of her is delicious…

"Eve, what have you done to me?" I growl.

My hand moves faster now, and I know it won't be long. I hold the image of my beautiful girl naked and spread out before me, her fingers spreading her pretty pink folds open for me.

Growling with desire, that image pushes me and I come hard and heavy. I quickly snatch the bedsheet to catch all of my cum, ribbons of it. My body shudders, hips rocking as I picture filling Eve with all my seed, to the point that it's leaking back out of her pussy. I can't wait to finally show her what it feels like to be flooded by a demon…not a fucking shifter. Fuck you, Dracon.

The thought of Dracon sliding his cock into her kills the moment instantly for me, and I snap open my eyes, pissed.

Right then, the phone beeps with a message, vibrating on my nightstand.

I glance over to it and snarl under my breath. Who the fuck is messaging me at this hour? It's not even eight a.m. My thoughts shift to joining Eve in her room instead.

I push out of bed and drag myself into the bathroom for a quick shower then return to my phone buzzing once again.

Rolling my eyes, I cross the room, snatch the phone, punch my pin, then swipe open the message. It's from an unknown number, so I tap it open.

There's an attached video and beneath it, the words, "I'm going to defile her, my friend. Just like you defiled my car. Enjoy the show you fucking demonic bastard."

My stomach hardens, panic gripping my heart, and I instantly stab play on the video. It opens and the first thing I see is Eve.

My heart constricts.

She's naked, tied up, and bleeding from cuts. Her head is tucked forward like she's unconscious.

The fuckhead, Dimitri, steps into the screen. He moves to her side and grabs her by the hair, fisting it, then wrenches her head back.

My chest constricts and I'm shaking with fury, squeezing the phone in my hand with rage.

She's out of it while the fucking bastard is groping his cock over his pants. Then he stares into the camera. "You fuck with me, and I'll bury you," he growls, then the video abruptly ends.

I roar, bellowing at the top of my lungs and hurl my phone across the room. A manic desperation consumes me and I'm ready to leap out of the window and go hunt her down. I sprint to go drag some clothes on, then snatch the phone—with a cracked screen—off the floor. It still works when I jab it with my finger.

Then I turn to the door and fly out, something inhuman reverberating from my chest.

I burst into the main room where Dracon and Knox are talking.

"Eve's gone. Dimitri took her," I growl, and saying the words out loud has my knees wobbling beneath me as I keep picturing her tied up and naked at his mercy.

He's going to rape her. I shudder with fury, fire inhaling my insides.

I don't hear their responses but I throw Dracon my phone. "He sent me a message. We need to go get her now. I'll burn down the whole fucking city to find her. Get your wings out, I need to find her fucking now!" I'm livid and I shove the whole couch out of my way, then kick over the table.

Both are watching the video, and I hear Dimitri's threat, the glee in his voice. A litany of swearing rushes past my lips as I approach them, my fists curling and uncurling.

Knox's gaze flicks around us, looking completely wild like a feral animal. Dracon's face tenses, his shoulders lifting just as he does before he shifts. He snaps his attention back at me, and he looks like the monster he is on the inside.

A growl rips from his throat, and he rushes past me, knocking into me in the process.

Knox and I pivot and lunge after him. "The fae prince dies today," I vow under my breath.

CHAPTER NINE

EVE

Someone shakes me back to consciousness by sheer brute force. My eyes fly open from the feel of the rusalka's hands on my face, grinning like a bitch, throttling me.

"Not sure she's fully awake yet," she says sarcastically, finally releasing me.

Still disoriented, I try to work out where I am and why in the world it feels like I've been run over by a truck. Moving is close to impossible as something bites into my wrists. I crane my neck up to find that my arms are tied to rope that hangs from the ceiling, and I gasp as I stare down to see I'm completely naked. My legs are wide, ankles bound to rope. I'm bleeding from at least half a dozen cuts and scratches over my body. Shit! The bitch stripped me then attacked me after I had passed out?

I jerk my gaze up just as a burst of icy water is thrown into my face. The cold jolts me totally awake.

"Fuck!" I cry out, my breaths rushing, thoughts flood

me. The kind where I want to destroy the bitch standing in front of me. The water is freezing and bites into my skin as it runs down my body.

The pathetic woman is holding onto a plastic bucket, chortling like a fucking pig. "Finally, she's awake," she purrs, looking away from me and to Dimitri, batting her eyes.

I stare at the asshole as my pulse thunders. He towers over me, his pale hair loose around his long face. Sharp features, the asshole is hypnotically beautiful… but isn't there a saying that the most beautiful things are also the deadliest?

His collar of tatts extend down his arms, visible under his rolled up sleeves. Fae power ripples off him, clawing into my flesh like acid. Considering how powerful the rusalka are, I don't want to discover what he's capable of. I know little about the fae beyond them being deceiving tricksters. Well, I can add lunatic and psychotic to that list.

"Let me go," I demand, sounding braver than I feel.

Only then do I really take in where I am—a barren room that might be basement, an abandoned home, or even Hell for all I know. Windows are bordered up and only the flicker of a single light bulb slices away the shadows. There's paint peeling off the walls, the floor is covered in trash, and a rat scurries right past Dimitri's feet. He kicks the rodent, then lifts his dark gaze to meet mine once more.

My throat tightens and I tug against the rope bound around my wrists. How many people have been tortured in here by this monster?

Every inch of me aches like I've been beaten while unconscious.

"Finish her," the woman screeches. "Or let me do it. She killed Mariana."

I hate her so much, and I want nothing more than to shove those words down her scrawny throat.

"She's mine," Dimitri's stony voice commands in a thick Russian accent.

"You're making a mistake," I interrupt the lovers' spat. "You want to hurt Cassius for what he did, but he won't give a shit what you do to me. I mean nothing to the Kings. I'm sure there are more creative ways you can get back at him. Fae are super intelligent I hear, and you look like a smart man."

Dimitri raises a busy eyebrow, his pointy ears seeming to pull back aggressively. Oh, he didn't like something I said.

"She addresses you so improperly." The woman glares at me with death in her eyes. "Let me teach her some manners, my prince."

Dimitri ignores her and steps toward me, slowly unbuckling his belt. The image sticks in my head like tar. "She'll beg me soon enough and cry out my name." He licks his lips, sliding his gaze down my naked body, and when he meets my eyes again, there's a smugness there.

"I prefer my females to be more perfect," he says. "Less...what's the English word? Round. But I can see the appeal."

"Fuck you," I spit, my voice rushed. I'm heaving for breath as panic crashes over me.

My breaths grow raspy and I'm doing my best to curl in on myself, which is close to impossible while I'm tied up. Trembling, I open myself up to my power, ready to bury this entire building with these two monsters and myself in it. Even if I can't control it, I don't give a shit. I want them to hurt, to pay for doing this to me.

Power zips through my veins like fire and the walls begin shaking, responding instantaneously to me. I grin.

Almost immediately, the soft tune of the rusalka fills the room, the hum deep in my soul. The wave of my power flatlines, stolen from me. I dig deeper, calling to it, but I can't think straight when that damn tune plays through my thoughts. It makes me forget things, luring me.

"Stop," I whimper. "Fucking stop it."

Her eyes darken, burning with retribution. She's enjoying every second of seeing me squirm.

With a click of Dimitri's fingers, the song ends. I shake the fog from my head.

"See, I can be cooperative. Now it's your turn," Dimitri says. "I knew you carried power the first time I met you. Impressive, but it's useless with me. I do wish we were back in my homeland. We could have so much fun with all the ways I could make you scream. All my toys are there." His lecherous smirk sickens me.

"Don't fucking touch me," I snap. "I will destroy you."

Pausing at my side, he runs the back of his knuckles across my cheek and I flinch. "I am a fae of my honor. I made Cassius a promise. Eye for an eye, and once I'm finished with you, he can have the scraps." His hand falls to my breast where he pinches my nipple, hard, and I try to bite back my pained cry.

"Oh, I should have guessed you were a screamer. Good, I like when they scream." His breath is slow, steady. He's calculating every word, every action.

"You sonofabitch!" I spit in his face, my breaths sawing in and out of my lungs.

The brute wipes his face with the sleeve of his shirt, sneering as his lips curl over perfectly white teeth.

"I want you to fight me as I fuck you. I'm sure you're used to that, being rutted by those Kings like a slut." He tears open the front of his pants and draws out a huge cock. It's already hard, and fuck me, but why is it so long? A whimper falls past my lips and I pull back, tugging against the restraints. My muscles ache and burn, my chest tightening.

This can't be happening. Please don't let this happen.

Revulsion burns inside me like acid, and I can't stop the tears from falling.

He looks at me with pity. I fucking loath him.

"I give you my word that if you don't survive, I'll bury your body rather than dispose of it. See, I'm not a complete monster."

"You're a fucking bastard. Dracon will murder you for hurting me." I drown in the searing blaze in my chest. "Don't you fucking touch me."

He laughs as he tugs on his lengthy cock. "Are you going to scream for me now?" His cold voice rings in my ears.

I'm shuddering, tears running down my face, and I

feel like I am about to hurl. The moment he takes a step closer, I scream just as my power bursts forward once more.

KNOX

*E*lectricity snaps across my spine.

Snap. Snap. Snap.

It comes again and I wrench myself backward, stumbling over my feet, my shoulder smacking into the elevator wall.

"What the fuck?" Cassius barks, glaring at me over his shoulder as he steps out of the elevator and onto the Tower's rooftop. Dracon looks back at me, too, eyebrow arched, studying me.

"What did you feel?" he commands.

Horsemen are connected and sense each other's power if we are in close proximity.

"Eve, I sense her power." My gut hardens and I bolt out of the elevator, still drowning in the bite of her power. It's sharp and leaves an aftertaste of something sweet on the back of my throat. I can't explain it, but it's unique to her.

"Where the fuck is she then?" Cassius demands, marching up to me, Dracon on my other side, both staring at me like starved hyenas.

"Back the fuck off and let me try to find her." I need them out of my face. I turn to look out over the sprawling city, her power still pulsing inside me like a beacon, scanning the skyscrapers, the nearly endless ocean of buildings stretching out to the woodlands in the far distance. I move quickly around the perimeter of the rooftop, following the power until the thumping pulse deepens.

"There," I state, pointing toward the south. "She's in that direction." Adrenaline spikes through me and I skim my fingers over my nape where my hairs are standing. "She's scared. I feel the desperation in her magic."

A dull coldness fills me, a longing ache that brings out my fury. Eve is my enemy, but if anyone's going to hurt her, it's going to be me. No one else gets to lay a hand on her. She's mine.

My heart sinks as I stare out into the city where she's all alone with that fucking fae. Flames dance in my chest as I keep picturing the video from Dimitri. I suck in the air, my insides flare with each inhale.

Spinning around to face the others, I tell them, "I have no idea how long she's got. We gotta go now."

Cassius's face pales and he nods, while Dracon's already stripping his shirt off. His shift into a monstrous dragon comes in seconds, but in that moment, seconds feel like minutes...like hours. His body stretches, skin splitting, and is replaced by black scales. Enormous wings breaking free from his back, expanding, blotting out the sun. He's massive, four paws tipped with deadly claws the color of midnight, and a thunderous roar rushes from his gaping mouth. Razor sharp teeth on show—the guy is fucking huge and impressive.

As an apex shifter, he's the ultimate predator capable

of shifting into any creature. Of course, he chooses the deadliest—a dragon. I would do the same if I was in his position. They are feared by all, and I grin, glad that he's on our side.

I pat the Mortem Blade at my side, already picturing how much I'll enjoy cutting off the fae's cock before I slam the blade into his heart. I want him to stare into my eyes as he dies and know that he's not coming back. I've heard the tales of fae returning from the dead with their magic. But not if I have anything to do with it.

"We're doing this," Cassius bellows, approaching Dracon in his scaly glory, except the bastard shoots up into the sky. "Are you fucking kidding? He's leaving us?" the demon growls.

I stare up into the sky, unsure what he's got planned. His dark, winged shape sweeps across the sky before he takes a sharp turn and comes back in our direction.

"What the fuck?" Cassius backs up. "What's he doing?"

My heart thunders. I'll admit there's nothing more thrilling than having this monstrous beast plunging back to earth, coming at you.

He's on us in seconds, and that's when I spot his talons extended and I know the plan. As does Cassius, but he still shouts, "Fuck you, Dracon, just get the hell down here so we can ride you."

One second we're on the rooftop, the next, claws snatch me around the middle and I'm swept up into the air with such brutality, that I lose my breath. And not much makes me lose my breath…well, except for Eve.

Memories of her crowd in on me, leaving me empty

and slightly afraid for her. With that, my insides tighten and my heartbeat spikes. I hate to admit it, but I need her back. I need to hear her voice, to see her glares, to watch her body moving when she storms away from me. Most of all, I need to work out the shit between us.

Thoughts of losing her have me tasting bile on the back of my throat. I don't care about anything but getting to her fast.

Frigid wind lashes over me, and I glance over to Cassius who's tense in Dracon's other paw, looking pissed as he holds on. He's yelling something but his words are stolen by the wind as we race through the city. Not to mention the constant up and down with each beat of Dracon's wings jolting us about.

It's not the most dignified ride, but it's fast, and I sure as fuck wouldn't want anyone riding me like a horse. Except Cassius might have a point here. How the hell am I supposed to tell Dracon where to go when he won't hear me?

I focus on the city below, holding onto Eve's power, which is fading fast. Then suddenly I sense a spike of her fiery power just below us, then it fades to nothing. I glance back to the derelict row of old apartment buildings.

She's there. Fuck me. She's back there.

I start whistling, not getting Dracon's attention. Desperate times call for desperate measures. Maneuvering in his clutch, I grab the normal blade from my belt and slash it in the underside of his paw.

He suddenly drops several feet and roars. Pivoting

his head in my direction, he glares down at me, eyes burning amber with flames.

"Down there," I yell, pointing back to the buildings.

Something must register in his dragon-brain, because we're suddenly swerving and spearing downward, my stomach rushing up my throat. Bitter air blasts against me and my heart thunders.

"Fuck yes!" I shout, my fingers curling around his claws to hold on.

Panic flares as the earth rushes up toward us, yet in a spectacular move, Dracon swings left and swoops up at the last second directly in front of the building. His claws unfurl without warning and suddenly I'm falling.

Shit. We're at least two stories off the ground. I hit the ground and fall to my knees, barely catching myself. Cassius does one better and pulls off the hero landing on one bent knee, hands on either side of him.

He smirks at me.

"Show off," I state.

"Okay, where is she?" Cassius demands, jumping to his feet.

I sense the last tendrils of her power lingering in the air and I run to the second building to my right, calling out to Cassius, "This way."

A few steps in, and a tremendous guttural screech pierces the air. I crane my head back, figuring Dracon's about to burn down the place or something.

Instead, there's another dragon in the air. I blink, unsure what I'm seeing at first, because this creature is smaller than Dracon, yet it's coming straight for him. What the hell?

Does he belong to Dimitri? Dragons are rare, so to see two creatures in the air together is beyond unusual.

Dracon rears back in midair, neck arched, then he juts it forward, mouth gaping wide. A storm of fire explodes from his mouth in a funnel, completely engulfing the newcomer. Even from down here, I feel the intensity of heat.

Well, that fucker didn't last long.

I throw myself toward the front doors Cassius has broken through, and I take one last look up. It just happens to be exactly when the smaller creature flies right through the flames, seemingly unscathed.

What the fuck?

The two of them clash in midair, and I know now we're running out of time because whatever the creature is, Dracon is going to have to find a way to destroy it.

I snap around and dart into the darkness behind Cassius.

He moves like a beast, slipping into shadows, vanishing so fast that I know he's got Eve's scent. I hear him inhaling deeply, then charging right past the stairs and breaking through a door at the end of the corridor.

I'm on his heels, moving like the wind, my mind crazy with the thought that we're too late. That the bastard took her from us...from me.

Agony roars through me, the threat of what state we'll find Eve in blinds me with rage.

Cassius doesn't pause, and I charge right behind him down a set of steps into the basement. Putrid smells assault me and the walls are filthy, covered in holes and graffiti. There's no stopping Cassius. With a growl, he slams shoulder-first into the only doorway at the base of the steps.

Wood snaps, shards splintering in every direction as the door rips free from its hinges, literally disintegrating from his assault.

I jolt inside, leaping over the mess, my insides twisting with agony. Scanning the grimy room, there's no sign of Dimitri, but that's when I see her.

My Eve.

Bruised, bleeding, and tears running down her cheeks. She's tied up just as I'd seen on the video. Her gaze clashes with mine.

"Knox. Cassius," she pleads, and I rush to her as Cassius leaps through a gaping hole in the brick wall, to chase Dimitri I assume.

My sights are set on Eve. I need to free her, to protect her.

She's heaving for breath, her chin trembling, and her cheeks are drenched in tears. The sickening images in my mind of what he did to Eve have my breaths shuddering.

"I've got you, little dove," I tell her and crouch down to undo the rope from around her bruised ankles.

Fury punches me, rage pummeling into me like waves, rising and rising. She doesn't flinch at my touch, doesn't cower, but I'm seething.

When I release her arms from the rope, she collapses into my arms. I hold onto her. "You're safe now, I promise you. Nothing will ever hurt you again. Not a fucking thing."

The way she looks at me guts me. She's trembling.

"Hold on for a moment," I say and quickly unbutton my shirt, taking it off. I wrap it around her shoulders and help her push each arm into the sleeves before I pull it around her fragile body.

"He got away," she mumbles, while I do up the buttons. She's swimming in the shirt that falls down to just over her knees.

"Cassius has gone after him," I explain. "Did he hurt you?" I tenderly cup my hands to the sides of her face, holding her, staring into the tear-filled eyes that break my heart.

She swallows and doesn't answer right away, but stares at the gaping hole in the wall that leads to darkness.

"Little dove, please. I'm going mental on the inside, thinking the worst. I have to know because it's going to destroy me."

Fresh tears fall down her cheeks and onto my fingers. "He didn't get a chance to rape me because he heard you arrive. But he touched me, and I hate him so much. I hate that I couldn't stop him. I hated feeling so weak when I've fought my whole life."

She bursts into a sob, and I pull her into my arms, lifting her off her feet. My insides feel as though they're splintering. Even with the relief that the bastard didn't rape her, him laying his hands on her burns through me. I'm going to chop his fucking hands off and feed them to him.

I hold her cradled against my chest and she curls in tight, her head tucked low. She's in shock, but she'll be okay, I know she will. Yet, my revenge against Dimitri will be unexpected. My heart beats like a sledgehammer in my chest with anger, with revenge, with the pain at seeing Eve so broken.

"I'm going to make sure he suffers. I'm sorry we didn't get to you earlier, but I promise you, little dove, that everything will be alright again."

She holds onto me, and feeling her shaking against me hurts me. For a long time, I didn't believe I could feel anything for anyone. I told myself my heart was dead, but now my pulse thumps with agony at seeing Eve like this.

Heavy footsteps move in the room behind me, and I turn to find Cassius rushing over to us, his eyes black as coal. He looks very much like his demon but the moment he lays eyes on Eve, that side of him recedes.

His eyes are wide now, face growing paler. "Eve." His voice cracks and he's in front of us in seconds. He brushes the hair off her face as she turns to him, attempting to smile. It comes across pained.

"Did you find him?" she croaks.

"I'm sorry, gorgeous. I couldn't. He's gone."

I grit my teeth at the news, while Cassius strokes her face and wipes away her tears, telling her she'll be safe now. But a hungry desperation grows with me. A vengeful sensation that brings with it a darkness closing in around me that needs to make Dimitri suffer.

I'm clear on exactly what needs to happen. How I will spend eternity to find him if I have to.

"Knox." Cassius nudges my arms. "Did you hear me? Let's get out of here. And where the hell is Dracon?"

"Oh, right. He's outside fighting another dragon."

"What?" Eve and Cassius blurt out simultaneously.

"I think it's a dragon. I don't fucking know."

We rush outside, Eve still in my arms as I'm not ready to release her or have her too far from me until I know we're safe in the Tower. What I do know is that we're going to be installing magic security against the fae.

Stepping outside, I blink against the sunlight and lower Eve to her feet beside me. I wrap an arm around her waist, drawing her against me, needing her close.

I glance up into the sky just as the smaller dragon whips around, whacking his spiked tail right into Dracon's face. It's forceful enough to send him plunging toward the ground in a wild spin.

Eve screams just as he hits the ground behind the apartment in front of us, a puff of dust billowing outward from the impact.

Cassius growls, sprinting to where Dracon fell. I pull Eve back into my arms and run madly.

"Oh shit, what the hell is that?" she points to the sky, and I look up at the almost reptilian looking dragon circling higher above. Then, without warning, it coils around and zips across the sky, vanishing behind the billowing clouds in the distance.

"I'm guessing it belongs to Dimitri," I say, breathing heavily as I close the distance toward where Dracon fell.

He lies in front of another derelict building in his human form, growling with agony. Naked and bruised. His body is battered, but that's nothing new for him. Yet the injury from the other dragon's tail is something new, the side of his face red and swollen.

"Put me down," Eve demands, and I do as she asks. She rushes over to Dracon and kneels by his side, tenderly touching him, whispering things to him.

Cassius and I are there, crouching by his side. He's not dead, which is a good sign.

"What the fuck was that thing that attacked you?" Cassius asks.

I keep staring at Dracon's wound, how his veins seem to bulge around the red, inflamed cheek. This isn't a normal reaction from a strike. "I think you've been poisoned," I state.

Dracon groans and turns to Eve, not seeming to hear Cassius or me. He's holding onto her arm, asking her if she's hurt.

"I'm okay, but you're really hurt," she murmurs, skimming her fingers around his injury. I might have smiled at her affection if I wasn't consumed by fury.

Cassius's phone dings and he looks at it then back at us. "Taliah's here with the car. Let's get you both home."

The two of us pull Dracon to his feet swiftly where he stumbles.

Eve studies him with widening eyes. "Dracon, are you really poisoned?" She glances from him to me and back to the Alpha.

My breath catches as I stare at the agony on her face, amazed at how much she cares for him. Would she stare at me with so much devotion if something happened to me?

"It's a wyvern." Dracon forces the words through

clenched teeth as he throws an arm around Cassius's shoulders.

With Eve barefoot in a place littered with garbage and worse, I swing her back into my arms, enjoying the feel of her body against mine. She settles in nicely, placing an arm around my neck while turning her attention back to Dracon.

"What's a wyvern?" she asks as we hurry back around the building and make our way to the closest street.

Dracon doesn't respond right away, and he's rasping for breath. "Cousins to dragons, smaller than us, and they can't wield a blaze." His voice is hoarse and deepening. "But they are immune to dragon fire. They're agile and carry venom in their barbed tails. And also, extremely rare. It must belong to Dimitri."

Eve tenses in my arms at the sound of his name. I hold her closer to me, knowing that Dracon's injury is a distraction from her own ordeal.

"Shit, so where do we get an antidote?" she finally asks.

"Let's just get out of here first," Cassius says, regularly checking the sky for another ambush.

"My body will fight it," Dracon groans. "I'm immune to it, but it will take a few days to heal." He growls with each step and is deteriorating fast.

Up ahead, a black 4WD pulls up by the curb, and Taliah's out of the driver's seat, rushing to open the doors for us.

In no time, we're all inside the car, Cassius in the front, and I'm in the back with Eve and Dracon cradled close. Something has me glancing back to where we'd come. Dimitri is on my mind. Is he still here, watching us? Or if he did run like a gutless fuckhead? Part of me toys with remaining behind to track the dickhead down.

But instead, I become aware of someone else standing right by the doors of the building Eve had been tortured in.

Aris.

He's just staring at us with an empty look on his face.

Coldness moves inside me. With it comes all the pain from our past and agony flares from memories of what he'd taken from me. For so long I'd hidden on Earth, and he'd finally tracked me down here to finish what he started.

Hate burns in my veins because I've been waiting for him, too.

He just stands there, looking confused while under the influence of magic, and yet he'd also been drawn to Eve's power. Just like I had.

A bitter assault of anger pulses within me as he does nothing but stare at us.

Fucking prick. I will make him hurt for killing my horse, Time, for forcing me to end up stuck on Earth to stop him from taking my Mortem Blade. I need to find the right moment to eliminate him without bringing the full force of the other horseman down on me.

The 4WD takes off and we're all thrown back into my seats. I holler with a howl at how wild Taliah is behind the wheel. Who would have guessed? She charges down the road like an expert, swerving past cars and maneuvering into the traffic with ease.

"Where the hell did you learn how to drive like that?" Cassius mutters, just as shocked as me.

But I can't get Aris out of my mind. I twist around and take one last glance back at the buildings only to find that he is gone.

I suck in a hard breath, knowing it's only a matter of time now before all hell's going to break loose. He's a horseman of the apocalypse after all, and impossible to restrain for long.

So, I have to be ready.

CHAPTER TEN

CASSIUS

*H*eat rises up my neck. I can't get the image out of my head of Knox carrying Eve—and him giving me a filthy glare when I insisted on carrying her back into the Tower. I have a right to be jealous considering I caught Knox holding her over the balcony just the other day, about to drop her to her death. Yet the crazy dick seems to have had a change of heart, suddenly smitten.

Though I know him well enough to realize that he might have a change of heart tomorrow.

"Where are we going?" Eve asks me, drawing my attention as I hold onto her hand, drawing her into the kitchen.

"To bandage you up, gorgeous." She's freshly showered and dressed in a black skirt and loose shirt hanging over her small frame. The cuts on her face are blushing pink, reminding me of how close I came to losing her. How easily that fuck-face-fae kidnapped her. Clenching my teeth, I hold back my fury, reserving it for when I catch up to him. I'll rip out his intestines and feed them back to him.

"In the kitchen?" she asks, eyeing me suspiciously and breaking me out of my thoughts. She gives me a lopsided grin like she's ready to laugh but still looks slightly confused. She stands there, her wet hair dripping on the tiled floor while staring at me with those soft eyes and vulnerable expression.

I pause with her near the island counter in the kitchen and lean in closer, wanting every inch of her against me. I want to hold her tight, push her into me so no one could ever harm her again.

But I know she's waiting for my response, so I give her one. "The new bandages are still sitting in the grocery bag in the kitchen. And I've decided to make you my famous Devil's Mac and Cheese. Two birds, one stone." I grin, coaxing a small smile from this beauty.

"You cook?" She raises an eyebrow.

She makes me laugh out loud. "Why? A demon can't cook?"

"Well, just that I haven't seen you really eat."

"Doesn't mean anything. Human food doesn't fill me up, but I can appreciate a tasty dish. Ask Dracon. He loves my cooking."

Her gaze remains on me, narrowing with disbelief.

I slide my hands to her waist and lift her easily, sitting her on the counter. Her breath catches.

I do enjoy the small sounds she makes.

She's now at eye level with me, and I lean in and set my hands on either side of her silky thighs. "How are you feeling? Dimitri pulled a fucked-up move on you and don't worry, he'll pay, but I need to make sure you're okay."

It's ridiculous how much she fascinates me. I notice the small things, like how her pupils dilate from surprises, how the bridge of her nose creases slightly when she gets mad. And those lips have a language of their own, letting me know instantly how she's feeling. Like right now, they're tight at the corners, but not thinning, which means she wants to talk but is holding back.

"I think I'm alright," she finally answers with a soft whisper.

Sliding my hand up to her cheek, I cup the side of her face tenderly. "I'm sorry you went through that today. If I could, I'd take your place in a heartbeat. Seeing you tied up that way killed me."

She leans into my touch.

I scoot closer to her, my stomach pressed up against her bent knees. My touch has the desired effect of eliciting another smile from her.

"Shock can be a real kick in the teeth," I say. "I learned the hard way when I killed my first demon at the age of eight. It is a requirement to battle a monster twice our size to be accepted in society down in Hell, but apparently I didn't get the memo it wasn't a fight to the death, so I went wild and killed the thing. One moment the beast was alive, and the next, I had him on the ground and I was swimming in his blood. I did too good a job because from that day on, everyone was afraid of me, and growing up in a demonic city without friends is fucking hard. I suffered for a long time."

"I've never heard you talking about where you're from. Thank you." Her eyes glint with genuine interest. That's new. Especially since no one asks about my past. Ever.

"Well, today is your lucky day. I'm in a sharing mood." As much as my instincts scream at me to thread my fingers through her wet hair, promising she will never be in pain again, I break away from her. Something must be royally broken inside me. I don't do soft gooey emotions. I'm a fucking ferocious demon who can barely control my monstrous side and yet, around her, I am tame.

"Make yourself comfy," I say, striding across the room to collect the unpacked bandages. I'd asked Taliah to pick up a bunch after the incident Eve ended up covered in venomous snake-shifter blood.

While the three of us Kings heal on our own, Eve is a different story, and that means having items in the Tower she needs.

Pawing through the bag, I grab several different sized boxes of bandages and antiseptic cream when I spot a packet of tampons at the bottom of the bag, along with something called a menstrual cup. What the hell is that?

I take the whole bag with me to Eve and set them down next to her. "Taliah got you some items too," I say, watching Eve open up the bag.

A droplet of water runs from her temple to her jaw, where it splashes onto her cleavage. My thoughts drown in images of her dusty pink nipples, at how responsive they are to my touch. Instantly my cock responds with a twitch.

Lifting my gaze, I notice she's watching me and says, "Why are you looking at me so strangely? Are you uncomfortable with feminine hygiene?"

I pull my shoulders back, needing to get my mind off her curvy tits and back to what she's talking about. Oh right, the shopping bag. "Quite the opposite. If you'll let me, I want to be the one to use them on you. To watch you." I mean every damn word. "Blood doesn't scare me."

I stare at her piercing green eyes, knowing I've caught her off guard by the way she's nibbling on the corner of her mouth, actually considering my offer. There goes my cock hardening even more.

"You surprise me a lot," she says. "But, if you're curious, one day I'll show you." Her grin is wicked, like the idea excites her as much as it does me.

"And the cup? I'm confused about how that works. Will you show me that, too?"

She laughs that time, and I swear she's blushing. Adorable. "To be honest, I've never used one, but I have a general gist of how it works."

I rip open one of the bandage boxes and unscrew the antiseptic cream before squeezing out a dollop onto some clean gauze. "I'll hold you to your word."

Everything about Eve is temptation. Normally, I'm up to my neck in dealing with crap, yet when she's in my presence, I can only focus on one thing...her.

Another droplet of water trickles down the side of

her face, and she wipes it away. The atmosphere thickens while desire claws at my chest.

I smear the cream across the deep lesion on her collarbone. She winces, holding back a whimper. Then I place a bandage over it.

"Why are you suddenly being so nice to me?" she asks, holding my gaze when I raise my head.

"Haven't I always been nice to you?"

Her laughter answers me. "Nope. I'm guessing you're feeling guilty for Dimitri punishing me to get back at you, aren't you?"

I swallow hard and watch the way she holds a straight face as she speaks the brutal truth. Fuck, her words jab me right in the chest, and my heart feels like it's wrapped in barbed wire. Guilt's chewing me up badly, I can't deny it.

"You're right," I answer. "I feel like a piece of shit that they used you to get to me. But do I regret defiling that dickhead's car? Not a fucking inch. I know that's not what you wanna hear."

"Not really. But in truth, I wish I would have slashed his tires at the party." She laughs, the sound flooding me with excitement. I keep disinfecting her cuts and bandaging them, a sense of calm coming over me. She deserves everything, and I doubt I can ever make up for what happened to her because of me. I'll grovel, give her the world on a platter. I feel like the worst fucking person in the world.

How could I have been so stupid to not have realized he might target her to get to me. I tense, fury bleeding into my veins.

Looking her up and down, and at the half-dozen bandages across her body, something shifts within me. She brings out something in me…something primal, starved, possessive. The need to own her is destroying me.

I need to keep that dark shit in my head, so I do my best to change my tune and not freak her out. "Where else are you hurt?"

She lowers her gaze and tugs up her skirt up to her bikini line to reveal a knife wound across the top of her thigh. It pebbles with blood instantly. "This one's been stinging."

It's not a deep, but enough to hurt. She doesn't seem to shy away from the fact that she's flashing me her black panties, and I suspect she's doing it on purpose to get a reaction out of me.

And it's working because I crave this girl. I want her.

On my cock.

Beneath me.

Against the wall.

On her knees.

But most of all, screaming my name.

I remind myself that getting close won't end well…I bring only death to those in my life. Truthfully, I need an outlet for all the crap in my head and my past before I explode.

But Eve…she's something special, isn't she? Sometimes it scares me how quickly I'm losing my damn mind. I shake the thoughts from my head and notice her studying me.

Lowering my attention once more to her flashing

me, I say, "So, you're back to wearing underwear again." I smear the cream over her wound. "We might start up a no-panty rule in the Tower." I grin as I meet her gaze, imagining her bending over and flashing me. I get light-headed from how fast the blood dives south to my strangled cock.

"Yeah, right," she gasps. "Then you three would have to follow the same rule." She leans back on her hands on the counter as I layer a bandage across her thigh, my fingers tracing between her gorgeous legs. Her skin is extremely soft and it's so warm. As much as I try, my gaze keeps dropping to the thin fabric keeping me away from her delicious little pussy.

I slowly slide my fingers to the inside of her thigh and her breath catches at my touch. Captivating.

"I can't speak for others, but I always go commando. Maybe you should try it out." The mental image of her scorches my mind.

"I don't think so." Her voice is strong, yet she smirks.

"I'm not saying I'll do anything but look."

"Right. I can see it in your eyes. You can't control yourself, just like back in the parking area that landed us in all this trouble."

"You're killing me with guilt," I murmur. "But it doesn't stop me from wanting your underwear off."

She laughs at me. "You're persistent."

I haven't been able to get her out of my head since she infiltrated my life. I need this girl. To fuck her. To bury myself deep inside her and stay there until I flood her with my seed.

"When it comes to you, I have little control. I'm not good at not getting my way."

"It's a trait all three of you Kings share." She leans back on bent elbows, leaving her skirt hiked up, the invitation clear.

I study her, convinced she's playing at something, but I blow that thought aside. I can't take my eyes off the sheer fabric where I can clearly see every curve, every crease of her pussy. I'm completely captivated.

If my little Eve wants me to distract her, then I'll give it to her. Whatever she wants, especially if it puts a dent in the guilt swallowing me alive.

My palms slide up the sides of her legs while holding her gaze. She smirks at me. Sliding under her skirt, my fingers coil around the elastic of her thong at her hips. I snap the thin fabric.

She groans, acting all surprised and wide-eyed, pulling herself back up.

"Don't pretend you didn't know what you were doing, beautiful one." I grab the torn thong and rip it completely off her.

She presses her thighs together, but not before I catch a glimpse of her pink morsel. Her sweet scent floods my nostrils, and my hands are back on her thighs.

"Is this what you want?" I ask, my fingers pressing into her legs, my cock stiff in my pants.

"Depends on what you're offering," she teases, having no idea what she's getting herself into because I'm too far gone now. Committed, and there's no turning back.

I lick my lips while prying open her thighs. There's little resistance, and I lower my gaze to her sweet lips, already glistening.

Fuck me, this girl.

I swallow hard and move my hands to her hips and haul her ass to the edge of the counter.

"I own every inch of you," I say, my gaze flaring as she widens her legs on her own, her gorgeous lips spreading, showing me everything. "Your pussy is fucking beautiful."

Her chest is rising and falling quicker now, her breaths shallow. Her cheeks flush red, and I run a finger down the middle of her slick. She's burning hot and so wet. Maybe it's fate that she's openly giving herself to me and not fighting me. Like we are meant to be.

She stares at me half-excited, half-nervous by the way she keeps tugging her bottom lip into her mouth.

"I need to hear the words, Eve. Tell me what you want from me." I won't push her, not today, not after what she went through. But if she needs this, then I'll worship her.

"Please, Cassius, I want to feel good about myself. I want this, I need you."

"Oh, Eve, you have no idea what spell you've put over me. I'd walk on shards of glass if it brought you relief from what you went through. I'll take care of you."

Even before I place a kiss on her inner thigh, I know she's mine. After today, there isn't any doubt in my mind that I will keep her forever.

When I push a finger into her, one inch at a time, her

eyes flare with arousal, her pussy sucking down on my fingers as I press in another.

"Is this what you want?"

"Yes, oh god, yes." Her eyelids flutter as her eyes haze over.

"You can use me anytime." Not waiting for her response, I press my lips to her pussy, my tongue lapping her, flicking across her clit.

She's arching her back, moaning, bringing out a fierceness to hold onto her.

Her taste is pure intoxication, and I rub my mouth over her, needing her all over me, drowning in her scent. I run my tongue the full length of her slit. She rides my face, grinding herself against my tongue.

There's absolute beauty in seeing a woman aroused. Listening to her, watching her, completely strips me raw—it obliterates me.

My cock's so hard it's painful. I ravage her, coaxing louder groans out of her. If Dracon hears her while he's in his room, recovering from his poisoning, that's not my problem. And who the fuck knows where Knox is, as he marched out of the Tower, saying he had shit to deal with almost as soon as we got back.

More Eve for me.

Her groans escalate and I enjoy every lick, every nip, savage pleasure igniting within me. She rocks her hips, grating them, and I place her legs over my shoulders, making her more comfortable.

It's only when I feel her legs trembling that I know she's on the edge.

"Cassius," she cries out, and I want more, to hear my

name on her lips every fucking day. I never slow down, but I slip my tongue into her, curling it to drive her wild. She's louder now, and I press my nose to her clit, giving her everything.

Her fingers spear through my hair, and when I look up, her sexy gaze finds mine. I give her a wink, and pull my tongue out, eating her with addiction.

"Please, more…" Her words morph into a scream as she convulses beneath me. I lick her faster, take her pussy into my mouth, and lap up everything she gives me.

Shuddering, she thrashes as her body trembles with her arousal.

Fucking stunning.

Something rattles in my chest with complete satisfaction at hearing her cry out. I hold onto her hips, not letting her get away until she's completely undone.

Breathing heavily, she collapses slack on the counter, and only then do I release her. Standing, I stare down at my grinning goddess.

"That was amazing," she exhales.

Staring at her in utter bliss, her cheeks flushed, her eyes alive, and her legs spread before me, she is the epitome of perfection. If I thought I was lost before, now I know I'm completely in over my head.

I draw her into my arms, feeling her tits, her legs wrapping around my waist.

"It seems we have a problem." She moans. "You're still wearing your pants."

"Today's not about me, but you." I thread my fingers through her hair and kiss her. The kind of kiss where I claim her, plunge my tongue into her mouth so she has no room to doubt my feelings for her. It's slow, but deep and calculated. Her hands grasp my shoulders, kissing me back with fire. With a passion I've never experienced with anyone else.

I already know that I'd take a bullet for her. Die for her. I don't care how crazy it sounds. I don't fucking care. I'm completely obsessed with this girl.

We break from our kiss, our breaths racing. "No one will ever hurt you again."

Her mouth pulls into a smile and she leans against me, her arms over my shoulders, and I hold her. Her body is so warm, fire between her legs, her delicious tits pressed between us.

Not wanting her far from me, I start collecting all the ingredients I need for my mac and cheese. She remains attached to me, and I fucking love it.

By some mastery on my part, I got the pasta boiling in milk and the four types of cheese ready for grating, along with a few spices that are my secret ingredients: cayenne, nutmeg, pepper, and a pinch of dry mustard.

"It smells good," Eve says, pulling away from me. She wriggles and I set her on her feet.

She watches me bring the meal together while I give her the grater and block of cheddar cheese. "Make yourself useful," I tease.

I prepare the brie, and quickly grate parmesan and then the cheese that makes all the difference. Gruyère cheese.

"This is a lot of cheese," she says. "My go to is box mac and cheese."

"Then be prepared to be blown away. Mine has a bit of heat to it."

Eve hops up on a stool by the island counter, and I get to finishing up the dish.

"So, what happened in Hell? Why did you leave?" she asks out of the blue, which I suspect has everything to do with me mentioning the past earlier.

I shrug because it's not something I talk about often to anyone. I guess if there's going to be any level of trust on her part, I ought to be truthful about the shitshow of my past.

"Are you sure you want to know? It's nothing glorious or heroic."

"That's okay," she answers. "Not like my upbringing was anything but crap. Not to mention a big chunk of my childhood I can't recall. And now I guess I know why. So, hit me with yours."

Adding the cheeses to the pasta, I figure why not share. It's what humans love to do. "In short, I had a fling with Lucifer's daughter the night before her arranged marriage, and we got busted by her father."

"Fuck," she murmurs. "Like Lucifer himself? Satan and all that?"

"Yep. He's everything the stories paint him to be. A real fuckhead. Anyway, that night my family and his got into a small war, and Lucifer was furious. After all, he just lost all his power connections to the family he was about to marry his daughter, Jenilf, into. See, the way it works in Hell, is that it's not Lucifer alone who holds all the power. There are at least a dozen powerful families who all control different realms and allegiances of the underworld. And building this alliance through marriage would have given Lucifer power over the Leishu world, where the most vicious monsters live, for him to use them as his warriors. Guess I fucked that up badly for him."

"Wow. Okay, so you ruined his plans. Then he kicked you out?"

"Not completely." I stir the mixture, throwing in more butter. "You see, Jenilf was obsessed with me, and I was a fucking bastard, wanting nothing but a fun night. I knew she was getting married, but I didn't care. Jenilf told her father she wouldn't marry anyone but me. She's his only daughter, you see, as he's only ever had sons. And I could see the train-wreck coming my way, so I made it clear I didn't want to marry her."

"Ouch."

"Yep. Lucifer was seething, and he set fire to half of Hell with his fury. And everyone blamed me. I was hunted, so I ran. But you can't get far from Lucifer in Hell. He eventually found me, and he tried really hard to kill me. Things don't die in hell, though, yet he fucking tried everything to eradicate me. When that didn't work, he ripped me away from my family, from my six brothers, from my friends, and hurled me out of Hell."

"Oh, shit."

"And the kicker is that if I ever return, he will torture my family and anyone I've ever associated with, for eternity."

She gasps. I don't look at her, as I refuse her pity. The past hammers into me—I knew that talking about my past would take a toll. My chest tightens from everything I've lost and left behind, of the family and friends I'll never see again, or a world where I'm ridiculed from the lies Lucifer spewed about me to save face. The shame I brought my parents.

I never planned for that. I'd been a fucking idiot, looking for a good time with a girl infatuated with me. That is why I keep my inner monster locked away. He's my past, a memory I've lost, not to mention he's still fucking furious. And I don't need my beast to accidently force open a portal to Hell to get revenge.

So, I live with only half of myself, while reminding myself that I'm doing the right thing. No matter the heartache and agony it brings me. I will suffer to never bring such danger to my family again.

Sighing, I turn back to the mac and cheese, then pour the mixture into a shallow dish before covering it with more cheese and spices. I pop it into the oven.

Chest tight, I turn to Eve, who's staring at me with huge eyes filled with sorrow. Agitation settles over me because I don't need her sadness, and yet the memory of my past is still vivid all these years later.

"It's okay, gorgeous. I've accepted my fate. I fucked up badly, and I have to pay the price. Earth is now my home. And the Kings are my new family." As much as I attempt to sound confident, my voice doesn't quite sound as strong as I'd hoped.

"I don't know what to say. And I thought I'd faced a terrible past. I'm so sorry, Cassius."

"Shit happens, and you adapt or it swallows you up. I fit here well. Dracon's and Knox's pasts are just as fucking broken as mine. It's why we fit together so well."

"Must be why I seem to fit in, too. It's a tower for broken things." She laughs and hops down from the stool. In a few steps, she's by my side, throwing her arms around my middle, hugging me, comforting me.

Okay, I wasn't expecting that. I don't push her away, but enjoy her against me. When was the last time someone hugged me for comfort? The sad thing is, I can't remember.

Heartbreak isn't a pretty thing. It's not like the humans portray on TV, staying up late and listening to sad songs and all that bullshit. It's completely losing your shit in the middle of a street when you least expect it. It's breaking down out of the blue from hearing a voice that reminds you of someone you lost. The memories still choke me, and sleep is impossible when the ache burrows deep into my soul.

The timer on the oven goes off and I flinch. I take the moment to break free and collect the finished dish. Besides, I'm tired of talking about myself.

"Okay, are you ready to taste the most incredible mac and cheese?" I change the topic, forcing a smile on my lips.

"Absolutely." She's back on her stool, and I set the baked dish on the counter in front of her, then serve her a small bowl. Handing over a fork, I lean on my elbows on the counter and watch eagerly, shoving every other thought to the darkest recesses of my mind.

She breathes in the baked smells with a smile curling on her mouth. Then she digs her fork in and scoops out a portion, the cheese stretching, before she blows on it. She pops it into her mouth, and I'm captivated. She makes a moaning sound, her shoulders sagging forward.

Her eyes travel up from the bowl and land on my face. She looks at me, shocked. Swallowing the mouthful, she digs for more, saying, "Holy crap, Cassius. This is incredible. Like, the most amazing thing I've ever tasted. I think I just had a second orgasm. Plus, the spice. I love that it has a tiny kick."

I laugh and keep admiring the way she eats. Of course, she'd like it. I made it.

"I seriously doubted you, but you proved me wrong."

"That's cute, but I know I did," I purr. The girl is spectacular, her skin kissable, her body all mine, but most of all, she's enjoying something I made for her. That lights me up from the inside out.

And the longer I watch her almost make love to the dish—already spooning more into her bowl—something else comes to mind.

For so long, I've held myself strong, taking cocaine to control my demon, and I've managed to keep it all together. Yeah, there are days I swear I'm going to lose it and succumb to my demon, to let my past destroy me. But I've worked hard at making those walls around me unbreakable.

Yet, the more time I spend with Eve, the more I'm beginning to think that she might just be the one to finally break me.

CHAPTER ELEVEN

Things are strange now… To be left alone in the Tower without anyone watching me closely. I'm not sure if I should take it as a compliment, a sign of their trust, or if it's because they think I've become too afraid to try and escape now. Complacent.

And maybe I have.

My run-in with the fae has shaken me more than I like to admit. I barely leave my room unless absolutely needed, and there's no way in hell I'll be leaving the Tower without at least one of the Kings with me. There are too many creatures out there who want to kill me or use me, and I'm not fucking stupid.

It's safer here, with them. As much as I may hate to admit it.

Staying put also means I'm bored most of the time. I pass the hours mostly practicing my floor routines for the magical day I can go back to my job at Kat's Kradle, or doing yoga. My entire life, I've been forced to keep going out of survival, and now that I can't go anywhere for that very same thing, I'm kind of...stumped.

So, you can imagine my excitement when I get a knock on my bedroom door and a familiar female's voice calls to me from the other side.

"Eve? It's Taliah. Do you have a—"

I throw open the door before she can even finish the sentence. She jerks back, surprised by my abruptness but smiles when she sees me.

"Hey," I say. My smile stretches across my face. "What's up?"

Her gaze quickly scans my room. Nervous-like. "I, uh, have some things here for you."

Wait... "Things?" I ask, confused. "What things?"

When I pull the door open more, I find a line of men dressed in uniform polos standing with a rack of clothing. There are about ten of them, lined up down the hallway like a parade. Before I can ask any more questions, the men start filing into my room, heading for the closet. They begin to open garment bags with beautiful, expensive dresses and perfectly tailored outfits, all designer brands and made with top-of-the-line fabrics. There are even accessories, shoes, purses, jewelry—it's a fashionista's wet dream come to life.

I watch, speechless, as Taliah comes to stand beside me in her typical pencil shirt and patterned blouse. We take in the excessive wardrobe being unwrapped and stocked into my small walk-in closet in silence. I'm not even sure how they're going to get everything to fit in there.

"What's this all about?" I ask.

"Dracon," is all she says, as if that'll be enough of an explanation. And it kinda is.

Dracon is always over-the-top with everything he does—killing people, his emotions, sex… So my guess is that he tried buying me a gift and, well, things got out of hand in typical Dracon fashion.

But what I really want to know is *why*. It's a super sweet gesture, and the man isn't actually the sweet kind.

Taliah must expect my question before I can ask it because she says, "After what you went through with the fae, he wanted to make sure you were taken care of."

The men continue to work like a well-oiled machine, opening bags, organizing the clothing into the overcrowded closet, and then placing the empty bags back on the racks. It's more clothes than I've seen in some department stores, let alone my own space.

"Taken care of, as in…" I begin.

"Happy," she says with a dip of her head.

It's hard to think of Dracon trying to make anyone happy but himself.

My chest warms. Dracon showing affection of any kind is so unheard of that it hits me differently. I thought I had him all figured out, but I wonder if there are more sides to him I still need to discover. Who knew the big, bad Apex was capable of softness.

"Ain't that the truth," Taliah says, and I blink at her, realizing I must've said that thought out loud. Then, we both burst out laughing.

It takes a bit, but once the men start to cart away the empty racks and leave us alone, we're finally able to catch our breath.

Taliah wipes actual tears from her eyes. "Man, I haven't laughed like that in a long time."

"You know what? Me neither," I say. It's true. I can't remember the last time I felt carefree enough to let loose. There's just too much shit going on in my life right now.

Walking over to my closet to check out my new spread, I wave for Taliah to join me.

I thumb through the luxury clothes and encourage her to look, too. She's hesitant at first, but eventually gives in and follows along.

Every piece I touch is luxurious, intricate, *expensive.* Swarovski crystals, silks, premium leathers, bright colors and patterns. I spot a price tag left on one of the black halter cocktail dresses and choke on my next breath.

Two thousand dollars? For a dress!

That's insane!

I had a fat bank account before the Kings torpedoed into my life, but I'd never dream of spending so much on one piece of clothing. Especially when most of my time was spent naked anyway. It didn't make sense.

Now, I had a closet stuffed to the max full of clothes fit for royalty. There had to be like a million dollars in there. Maybe two!

When I glance over at Taliah, I see she's having fun looking at all the pricey items, too. I notice her peek down at her own outfit and shake her head before going on, and a thought comes to me.

"Feel free to borrow whatever you'd like," I say, which makes her freeze on the spot.

"What? No. I couldn't. I—"

"You're a bit smaller than me size-wise, so some things may be too big—I got those birthing hips, you know. But I'm sure most of the dresses will fit you. Especially the form fitting ones."

She stares at me, as if she can't believe what I'm offering her. "But Dracon got these for you."

"And?" I chuckle. "Where am I going to wear this many fancy things? I barely leave my room."

Her smile stretches, lighting up her entire face. She's a very pretty girl, but it's obvious she has some confidence issues she needs to work out. Maybe I can help her with that.

I take her by the hand and pull her further inside. "Let's see what we can find." Skimming the different fabrics, I go back to that slinky little two-thousand-dollar cocktail number and pull it out. I hold it up to her and see that I was right—it'll fit her great.

"Oh no, no, no." She shakes her head adamantly, eyeing the price tag. "I can't. Dracon bought these for you. If he sees me wearing that, he'll lose his mind."

I wave my head. "You think he's going to remember every outfit he bought? There are over two hundred things in here. If he's like any man, he probably just handed the guy a credit card and said 'Have at it.'"

She laughs again. "You're probably right."

"The girls and I at Kat's Kradle use to share everything. Most of the time we couldn't even remember whose clothes belonged to who. Well, except bras. I'm more on the busty side."

Thinking about my old life with Demi and Mercy

and the other girls at Kat's makes a deep ache settle over my heart. I'm sure Kat's told them about me and how I've been mixed up with the Kings of Eden by now. Hell, she's probably told them about my powers and Aris. I couldn't see why not.

I bet they're all worried about me, wondering when I'll reach out, but as much as I want to, I don't know if I should. Just being my boss put Kat in extreme danger. I can only imagine what would happen if Franco or Aris found out that I had friends—if they hadn't already.

I shudder just thinking about it. I don't want anyone else harmed because of me, as much as I miss them and the way things used to be. I wouldn't risk their lives.

"If you're sure..." Hesitantly, Taliah takes the hanger from me.

"That's the spirit," I ease. "Besides, why not have some fun on the Kings' dime? Things have been so crazy lately, I could do with a little girl time. Let me do your makeup, too. Oh, and your curls are gorgeous!"

"I have to go pick up Dracon and Cassius in about an hour, but...what the hell! Let's do it." She squeals with excitement and twirls around, holding the dress against her body.

It may be silly, but I need this senseless fun, and it seems like Taliah does, too.

Besides, what is the harm in playing a little dress-up?

KNOX

*L*aughter rings from the other side of Eve's bedroom door.

Not just one person's laughter, either. There's someone else in there with her.

My body surges into action before my mind can think it through, and before I know it, I'm wedging my Mortem Blade between the door jam and the industrial metal lock Dracon had installed the last time Eve blew the door off the hinges, and shouldering the thing open. The walls shake from the force, plaster raining down all around me, but when I stand in the middle of the room and see Eve and Taliah there, wearing evening dresses and extravagant jewelry, my thoughts blank.

Their laughter stops abruptly, as if I've caught them doing something they shouldn't, and Taliah's face pales.

What the fuck...

"Knox!" Eve gasps with her hand over her heart. "Don't you know how to knock?"

I blink at her, confused by the question. "Of course, I do."

Her and Taliah exchange a look, and in their silence, my uncertainty grows. Taliah is our assistant, yet here she is dressed up with Eve, like they're about to go to another one of the Lord of Night's charity auctions. And looking guilty.

"I need to go...out," I say to Eve, choosing my words carefully, "and you're coming with me."

"Out where?"

"On an errand."

Her lips press into a thin line.

"You're not staying here alone."

"Right..." After another long bout of silence, she gestures to the short little black number she's wearing and says, "Can I wear this, or do I need to change?"

It takes everything in me to not have my gaze linger on the curves of her breasts or the way her hard nipples poke through the thin fabric.

I glance at the floor instead. "It doesn't matter. This will be a quick trip."

When Taliah and Eve meet eyes again, Taliah offers her a sympathetic smile. "It's okay, Eve. I'm just going to get changed back into my clothes and head out myself. I have to go meet Dracon and Cassius soon anyway."

"Okay."

That's good enough for me, so I turn and head out the door, down the hallway, and to the elevator. As expected, Eve follows me, now with a fur shawl wrapped around her shoulders, and together we ride the elevator to the ground floor. The moment we step out onto the sidewalk, a gust of freezing air smacks us both in the face, making Eve gasp.

"It's fucking freezing out here," she complains and shuffles close to me. "Shouldn't we take one of the cars or something? The limo?"

"The cold can't really touch me," I say with a shrug. "I usually just walk."

Actually, I fly around in my spirit form, but I'll stay in my human one for her. I just never considered taking one of the cars from the underground garage to avoid the winter temperatures. Then again, I don't know how these mortals drive these machines either, so I'm not sure I'd be able to operate one anyway.

"We'll make this quick," I say, noticing her shivering under the fur. "It's just a few blocks from here."

She hurries her steps in her high heels. I'm impressed at how well she can maneuver in those things. But I know as much about women's fashion as I know about driving.

Nothing.

All I do know is that her long legs sure look good in them. And the way it emphasizes her ass…

"Hurry up, Knox! It's freezing and I don't know where I'm going."

I hadn't even realized I'd fallen behind her. Distracted.

I shake my head to clear it. I need to stay focused on the job. Eve's too much of a distraction. She brings out urges in me that I shouldn't even have as a horseman.

And I don't like it.

I take the lead again and she manages to keep up with my pace, her heels clicking loudly against the sidewalk. Good thing I don't have to sneak up and get the jump on anyone tonight. It'd be impossible to keep us hidden; not with Eve. She's meant to stand out.

Swinging left between a quick-service laundromat and a closed-down storefront, we head to the back alley that runs behind the buildings and where all the garbage and recycle bins are stored for the block. The pavement is partly flooded here, and ice gathers in some places, which Eve watches for as she walks. The scents of putrefaction and raw sewage is stronger back here than the main street, and stray cats linger in the shadows, hoping to catch the rats that scurry out of their holes for scraps once night falls.

The meeting spot with Jericho is only a few more blocks up from here, but when the tingle of warning crawls across my neck, a shift in the Earth's very energy that promises death, I stop. My gaze swings over my shoulder and I scan the shadows, not seeing anyone but knowing they're there.

Eve halts too, coming up to my side. "What? What is it?" she asks in a quick whisper.

I hold up a finger to tell her to hold on, then close my eyes. I reach out with my energy, my power crawling along the ground like elongating shadows, scanning every inch.

"Knox?" Eve's worried voice buzzes in my ear.

When one of my spindles touches the pulsing energy of a living being, my eyes fly open, and she leaps back.

There you are.

I see you now.

"Stay here," I snap at her and shift into my ghost in the next second. Moving in this form is much easier, smoother, faster, and I can see things I can't while standing on two feet like a man. Like how every living creature on this plane produces its own aura of energy. It hums against my skin, calling to me, as if it's begging me to end it. Snuff it out.

And I see the man who's been following us immediately, ducked behind one of the large green bins made for recycling.

But he doesn't see me...

I'm on him in a blink, rising behind him like a nightmare come to life. He senses me and spins, just as my mortal body snaps into place again, and the fear in his eyes spikes my adrenaline.

I snatch him by the throat, lifting him off the ground. He sputters and coughs, his fingers clamping around my wrists and clawing for release, but I walk him into the middle of the alley as he curses in...*Russian.*

My anger tangles with my death lust. I recognize the language from our run-ins with Dimitri's gang in the past. He's tried to mess with Eve before, and it looks like me being with her this time isn't going to stop him from trying again. He even set his goon to stalk us.

That was a mistake.

Cassius and Dracon may have kept him alive, brought him back to my morgue in the Tower and had me torture him for information before killing him. But, unfortunately for him, he ran into me tonight, and I'd rather beat around the bush than go straight for the killing. It's more my style.

"Knox! What are you doing?" Eve cries, as the man's face turns a very pretty shade of purple.

"This one's been stalking us," I reply and give him a good shake. "He's one of Dimitri's."

She swallows hard, knowing what that means. He was coming for her. And just that thought has my blood boiling.

"What are we going to do with him?" she asks.

My gaze sweeps the skinny backstreet that's lined with the sad end of stores and restaurants, and finally rests on a small yellow storage shed behind the Chinese place. A perfect place to work my magic without being caught by a nosey passerby.

I carry the man over.

"Knox, what are you going to do?" she repeats her question, her climbing panic making her voice climb too.

What an odd question.

"I'm going to kill him, of course."

"Wait, what?" she asks me, breathing hard. "Here? Now?"

Her panic gets my blood pumping faster.

"Little dove, what you saw the other day at the Tower was just a taste of my darkness," I say, the hunger for death consuming me. "I think it's time I show you just how crazy I can be."

Suddenly the man's head swings to the side as he loses consciousness, and I drop him. His head hits the ground with a loud smack, and Eve flinches.

"Don't worry. He's still alive. For now." A quick glance left and then right, and I give the padlock on the shed's door a hard whack with my Mortem Blade and the metal breaks off easily. Banging my shoulder against the door, I drag the unconscious man inside and toss him onto the floor next to boxes of cleaning supplies.

Eve steps inside, peering over her shoulder nervously. "What if we're caught?" she whispers harshly.

I snort. I'm almost offended by her question, but then I remember she doesn't know how I work, that I'm a master of death in every way. Or how I don't leave fingerprints because I'm more phantom than human, and with our sway over most of Andover City's officials, we're basically untouchable by the law.

So, instead, I let her worry roll over me and move on to searching the shelves surrounding us for some fun things I can use to give this asshole a death that's much more spectacular than his pathetic life was.

I'll immortalize him through his demise.

Humming one of my favorite classical songs, "Für Elise" by Beethoven, I skim the jugs of bleach, drain clearer, and borax, my fingers wiggling with glee.

I'm in my element here.

Now what to pick... What to pick...

Oh, there's some home improvement-type stuff in here too. Paint remover, a plaster wall scraper—oh, that's sharp, I'll grab that. Could be useful. Some nails—always a plus. Pieces of pipe, a hammer—oooooo—a box cutter!

This is almost too easy!

I scoop a handful of goodies into my arms, carrying it over to the man slumped on the floor, and then dump everything by his feet. When I look over at Eve, she's staring at me with her mouth agape.

"If you want, you can wait outside," I say.

To my surprise, her lips snap closed and she shakes her head.

"Or, if you really want to, we can leave him here, so that when he wakes up, he can go tell Dimitri and he can send more fae after you. What do you think about that?"

The Russian groans, coming to.

"Better make your decision fast," I tell her. "He's waking up."

Sliding that plump bottom lip between her teeth, she stands up straighter, her chin held high. "Kill the bastard. I don't care."

The magic words.

And her staying put means that she wants to watch me do it, too.

A bolt of electricity zaps right to my groin and my cock hardens. Maybe she can be like us. A part of the Kings of Eden.

I'm excited to see just how far I can push the limits with her.

The man's eyelids flutter open, and his gaze jumps around the small room. He squeals and frantically kicks to push himself against a wall of shelves.

He'll really going to like this, then.

I snatch the box cutter off the shelf, flicking it so that the light catches the sharp edge and flashes diamonds across the filthy floor. Eve's eyes widen but she doesn't look away from me. And if she does, it's only to glance down at the outline of my cock pressing against my pants.

"Come closer," I say in an undertone. "Come and play with me, little dove. Unless you're scared?"

"Not scared," she whispers. "Just...curious."

Curious, I like.

"Then get on your knees."

The man lets loose a strangled sound of equal parts horror and disgust as Eve cautiously approaches me. She stops several inches away, close enough for me to see the tick of her heartbeat on the side of her neck.

"Now."

The demand has a rush of blood dotting the apples of her cheeks as she kneels in front of me, her hands loose at her sides. I run the blade over her lips expecting her to cringe. Expecting her to turn away from me in some kind of terror.

Trust Eve to blow my expectations away.

She lifts her gaze to mine, capturing my eyes, and darts her tongue out just as I pass the blade along her lower lip. Her eyes heat. Everything inside of me warms, my cock twitching and my heart thudding against my ribs.

"More," she demands.

I growl and grab the back of her hair to keep her in place while she tongue fucks the edge of the knife, fucking loving this. And me getting harder than I ever imagined at it. Then Eve slides her tongue along the edge of the knife and cuts herself.

Her gasp has me spasming as a drop of blood drops to the floor.

Instead of her shrinking away, she reaches out, still maintaining eye contact, and unzips my pants. She uses her other hand to free my cock from my boxers and the massive fucker springs out fast enough to hit her in the face.

I'm breathing heavy as she takes me into her mouth, painting my dick red with her blood. At the first suck, my eyes roll back in my head. Then I'm working her head with my grip, pumping her up and down on my cock and gagging her with it. The blood stains the length of me and drips on the floor.

"Oh yessss…" I hiss as my balls tighten. The pleasure

rolling through me is unlike anything I've ever experienced before. It makes me wonder why I've waited so long to have my little dove like this.

I grip the knife tighter. "That's right, little dove. Let me fuck your face. Let me paint *you*."

Lust riding me hard, I shift far enough to reach the guy. Cutting him across the cheek and listening to the music of his screams as blood wells.

Eve works me up and down, her cut tongue flicking across the underside of me while I press my palm to the man's blood.

"Fuck yes," I ground out.

I pull her off and she releases me, only long enough to smear the man's blood all over her chest. Pulling down her dress and painting those magnificent tits with it, I squeeze and knead them, and her head rolls back as I pinch her nipples. Hard. She's a masterpiece in red. She's sin and depravity and the answer to my goddamn dreams.

"More, Knox," she replies. "I want it to hurt."

Her words alone are almost enough to undo me. But I've waited too long to fuck her, and now that I have her here, no one's going to stop me. Not even myself.

Her chin, her neck, her chest, and my dick—they're all crimson.

And with the man screaming and trying not to look at us, it's like a dream from my deepest, darkest fantasies.

Reaching over Eve's shoulder, I grab a dirty rag from the shelf and stuff it into the Russian's mouth.

Oh, he's gonna watch.

The thought spurs me into action and I admit, I lose control. I yank Eve to her feet hard enough to have tears well in her eyes, my fingers knotted in her hair, and slam her back into the shelves. Then I steal the blood from her tongue in a searing kiss with my insistent dick pressed to her stomach.

Things rain down on the floor and hit our captive audience. I yank the dress from her torso, diving my fingers between her legs and finding her wet.

I'm ready to blow right then. Especially when she wraps her hand around my shaft and starts to work me up and down, using her blood as lube.

I'm kissing the air out of her lungs. I'm everywhere, my hands everywhere, her dress is tugged down to the waist, but I want more. I'm starved for her.

She presses her opposite palm against my chest, but not to send me away.

I haul her against me and pivot, slamming her back again, into the other side of the shed. Throwing her around like she weighs nothing. Eve wraps her legs around my waist to hold on. Panting and groaning and arching her hips in a clear demand to be fucked.

The Russian continues to howl through the material wedged in his mouth. With his death hanging in the air between us and his blood on her skin, I position myself against her pussy and surge inside.

Eve screams at the intrusion, followed by a low moan of pleasure. Her head tilts back, the edges of her golden hair covered in blood as well, her inner walls gripping me so tight that black spots dance in front of my eyes.

I fuck her with no remorse. I hate myself for wanting her like this, for giving into my primal, mortal urges, but I also hate myself for not indulging in her sooner. So, I fuck her through it all, pounding out my loathing and anger with every slam of my hips.

I like throwing her around. I like this Russian piece of shit watching me fuck her. I like fucking her the best, squeezing her softness until she tightens around me further. Coating her pussy walls with her own blood the way she did my dick.

I whirl around to drop her on her feet, silently urging her to widen her legs and spinning so that she faces the shelf this time. I hike up the dress higher, tearing her panties off her and exposing her ass completely.

I slam my hand down on her ass cheek, loving the sharp *crack* it makes and her gasp of surprise.

Not wasting another second, I press my dick to her pussy once again and resume my pace. My balls tighten and my orgasm builds.

"You're going to watch me cum all over her," I groan, watching as the Russian tries to close his eyes. I swing the razor again, cutting his cheek again. He cries out as more blood slides down his skin and those glorious lines of crimson drip down to his shirt.

"I said watch me, or I'll scoop your eyeballs out with a spoon instead."

He opens his eyes wide, pinning his stare on me.
Yes.

"You're going to watch, fucker, and when you die it's going to be so goddamn sweet."

Eve is panting, moaning, my name a prayer on her lips.

"Knox..." she moans. "God..."

Her pussy clenches around me as she cums, and my mind whirls. She's so tight, so perfect for me.

"My little dove," I whisper against her ear as I reach around and press my thumb against her clit. I stroke in time with my thrusts, riding out her orgasm until she's shuddering against me. When her knees give out, I wrap my arm around her middle to keep her upright and bouncing on my cock.

As much as I want to, I can't hold back any longer. My orgasm rips through me, and I throw my head back as my spirit tries to float from my body. Everything is heightened—the pleasure, the pain, the delicious sensations rocketing through me.

It takes a while for me to come down from the high, but when my spirit meets with my body again, I release her, breathing hard, grip the razor and slash it against the Russian's throat.

CHAPTER TWELVE

DRACON

For days now, something feels like it's been building up, like a tempest that will rip apart everything in its path. Something is coming... something fucked up.

Cassius doesn't seem to notice, as he's too preoccupied being obsessed with Eve. Whether he'd admit it or not, out of the three of us, he wears his heart on his sleeve, even if he doesn't realize it. He's like a broken vessel who's been desperate to find a way to put himself back together again. And Eve gives him that chance.

Someone once said to me that those with the strongest hearts have the most scars.

We don't talk about our pasts often because we're heavily scared by the shit we've been through. So, we look forward, not backward, to make it through each day.

I can't blame Cassius's obsession though. Everything about Eve provokes me, too, the beast within me roars for her. Lately, she's infiltrated my dreams and I wake up with her name on my lips, my lust for her in my hard cock.

A nerve twitches at my temple from how much I've let my own infatuation grow. Nothing good can come of it.

Night cloaks the city and my reflection glints back at me in the window. The gash across my neck still pulses red from the wyvern attack days ago. Those creatures are rare, and deadly as fuck. Their venom might not kill me, yet it lingers. I'm almost healed, though the scarring takes longer. Anyone else would have died within minutes.

Dimitri surprised me with his damn wyvern, he got the upper hand, and the fuckers escaped. Next time, I'll be better prepared.

Light footsteps tap the floor behind me, and I twist around to find Taliah. At my nod, she approaches, dressed in a tight pencil skirt to her knees, heels, and a tight button-up white shirt. Unlike Eve, she lacks in the curve department and is on the skinnier side, which isn't to my taste. Hair pulled back into a ponytail, her face is serious. I could give her more authority, rather than treat her as my servant, like I've done for the past five years that she's been my personal assistant. I did it on purpose as I worried about loyalty. I do it with everyone around me. But she's never once let me down.

Some days I feel sorry for her. She finished college with huge loans to pay off, but when she applied for the job, I discovered she had a stalker. A real fucking basket-case of a psycho breaking into her house to spy on her. She lived alone and was petrified. So I eliminated the bastard and brought here to work for me. And she's stayed ever since, so I keep her protected, pay her well, and ensure she's got everything she needs. Though I see sometimes in her eyes that she's ready for more responsibility.

"What have you got for me?" I ask, moving over to the bar to pour myself a glass of whiskey.

"Nothing good, unfortunately," she says, coming over to join me by the bar. She hops up on a stool and crosses her legs. I sit on the one next to her and take a sip from my drink.

"Go on," I say, ready for whatever the storm is about to unleash.

"The scouts have all checked in with me, and it's dead quiet on the streets. There's no sign of Franco or Dimitri. They haven't been seen for close to a week."

"That's fucked. Could they be collaborating?" I murmur, mostly to myself.

"Seems unlikely. All the Black Spades' men are gone from their usual places they hang out, too. Something's definitely happening."

The mood grows somber, and I down the rest of the whiskey, the heat pleasant on my throat, yet the ominous sensation closes in around me. I hate not knowing what's going on in my own backyard. That's not how wars are won.

I clench my jaw, my chest burning. What the fuck are they up to? I jerk my gaze to the bottle of half-empty whiskey, lost in my thoughts. "I don't remember the last time the streets were abandoned this way."

Setting the empty glass on the bar with a thud, I rise

to my feet, furrowing my brow. Franco always moves his men around in an attempt to not fall into routine for anyone watching them. That is normal, but his minions were always around. Always watching everything. And Dimitri, well fuck. He's not usually in my city. He'd just gotten out of prison so I haven't had time to look into who his alliances are with yet.

"Send the scouts out once more," I command. "Get them to sweep the streets, places they don't normally check. The roaches are close, and we need to find them. Cassius will help, as some of the scouts barely have two brain cells between their ears." Everyone takes the easiest path if there's a chance of getting away with it.

"Sure, I can do that. Whatever you need, I'll get it done," she says, sliding off the stool.

She bows her head in a show of respect, then retreats from the room with hurried steps.

I'm on the move too, unable to stand still, the fast angry thump of my heart pounding in my chest.

I don't do well with being kept in the dark. And if the asshole gangs are covering something, I'll find it before they strike. Rushing into the elevator, I pace as the car descends, agitated, not trusting that our scouts are doing enough.

There's only one solution. Sometimes you gotta get your hands dirty.

I strip, my clothes falling down around my feet. And when the elevator doors open, I launch out in my wolf form. Black as midnight, my fur ruffles across my nape with fury, with anticipation of uncovering what's been going on in my city.

A growl scratches over my throat as I approach my guards at the back door. They hastily unlock it and I lunge outside into the balmy night.

I pound my paws onto the pavement and pivot toward the back streets with fewer lights, where scum hang out. A gust of wind tosses garbage across my path. I take in everything, the world around me crisp and sharp. Voices play on the wind, music, smells of food. In the night, I see every shadow, sense every movement.

The thump of boots echo from a backyard I pass. I dart behind a trashcan and peer out as two men stumble out from the fenced doorway. The air reeks of alcohol, and they're drinking beer from bottles in brown paper bags, stumbling down the way I'd come.

Pisspots. Nothing more.

I race forward. Darkness crowds around me the farther I travel. As Taliah said, all the usual spots are dead empty. Even the clubs where they hang out show no signs of the lingering guards from the Black Spades. What the hell is Franco up to?

A muffled cry is abruptly cut off, followed by laughter. I keep going, racing through the city, and the farther I travel, the more my gut tightens.

What am I missing?

I'm trotting down a lone back street with only a flickering streetlight and broken cars for company when the wisp of long black hair from under a man's hood catches my attention. Something about the way he swaggers causally and with a slight limp on his left leg, his shoulders pulled forward, reminds me instantly of Saxon.

I do my best to ignore the voice in my head panicking that somehow it's him. Of course it's not, yet I find myself moving up closer to him through the shadows to double check.

An ache tears through me, memories I'd buried keep resurfacing. Keep reminding me of how I'd fucked up, how I couldn't do enough to save my closest friend. The man I considered a brother is dead, and every time I think of him, I break. The sensation is raw and rips me to shreds, feeling like it just happened.

We'd often run these streets in our wolf forms, unstoppable, and when the enemy saw us approach, they scattered like rats. Saxon was a berserker at heart. He fought like a beast, and even I had no chance of stopping him.

I tense all over, the memories swallowing me, drowning me. My thoughts come and go. *Don't think about it.*

I move on fast paws to catch up to the man strolling in the dark street. Not even bothering to conceal myself as I dart in front of him, turn and pause, staring up.

It's fucking stupid, but a desperate part of me holds onto the hope that it's Saxon…but when I look into the longer face, at the beady eyes, at the man who isn't Saxon, my heart sinks.

He screams suddenly, backpedaling, his eyes growing huge. "W-Wolf!" he bellows, then turns and runs toward the closest apartment building.

Fuck. What is wrong with me?

Holding onto such hope after all these years.

I retreat, ignoring the laughter in my head at myself,

at how much more broken I am than Knox, that I live with such delusions.

I'm suddenly running, hitting the ground hard with my paws, not pausing, letting the wind tear at my fur, wanting to feel my heart slamming in my ribcage. Anything but the shattering emptiness inside me.

Desperation clenches my throat, and I have no idea where I'm going, but I can't stop. I refuse to stop. I hate losing myself like this. *Fuck. Fuck. Fuck.*

I don't know how long I've been running, but the moment I inhale the stench of death, I slow down and backtrack. That's when I spy the figure stepping out of the shadows. The silvery light of the moon shines in his eyes, swallowing the stormy blue color.

Vampire. I growl and approach him, inhaling the air once more, getting a better indication of who I'm dealing with.

Alec—one of the Lords of Night and right-hand man to his leader, Marius. His loyalty to Marius is unmatched, and anything he sees and hears go straight to the other three Lords.

I shift back into my human form as I approach him, my fur retracting, my bones stretching, cracking, skin spreading over my body.

Cracking my neck, I inhale the gritty air, the pollution, layered with the vamp's smell of death. "Alec," I state. "What brings you to this side of the city?"

He grins, standing casually as he rubs his shadowed stubble. His dark hair sits messily around his face like it always does.

He stares up into the sky. "I'm picking up something." Then he lowers his piercing gaze to the small storefront behind him, no lights on inside, and back at me. "And you? I haven't seen you on the streets since you ruled with Saxon by your side." His nostrils flare, his words purposefully poignant and meant to be sharp.

"I needed fresh air," I rebut instantly. "So, Marius sent his loyal servant out on a retrieval mission?" I ask, mockery evident in my tone.

A glint flashes behind his eyes. If he attacked, I wouldn't see him coming until he struck. But the Lords don't scare me. Not a fucking inch. What scared me now is not seeing what was coming for us from the gangs who've gone into hiding.

Just then, an old, graying man emerges from the darkened store behind Alec and hands him a small parcel the size of my fist, wrapped up in a linen cloth. He lifts his head momentarily, meeting my gaze. Terror flares behind his eyes at seeing me. Quickly, he hurries back inside. The distinct snap of the lock sounds.

Alec hastily tucked the package into his coat's pocket. "Always a pleasure, Dracon."

He turns away from me, but I decide that if the other packs are going underground, maybe building my own allegiance isn't such a bad thing.

"Alec," I call out, to which the vamp twists on his heel to look at me. He doesn't say a word, but his impatience is scribbled across his face.

"Just a head's up. Black Spades and the Russians might be planning something. They've all vanished off the streets, so something is building. It might impact the Lords, too."

He nods, but his mouth is tight. "Thanks for the tip." Then he throws himself forward and vanishes in the blink of an eye into the shadows. Vampires are the shadows of our city, vanishing so fast, you never know they're there in the first place. Their scent gives them away to me, but to most humans, they're undetectable. It's why their leader, Marius, needs to keep such a tight hold over his coven and rogue vamps. If they run amuck, the carnage they'd leave behind would bring the city to its knees.

Curiosity burrows through me about what exactly Alec bought from a store that always looks shut down. Regardless, I throw myself back into my wolf form and dart into the night, needing to find out what the fuck Franco and Dimitri are up to.

They are my priority right now. Not the Lords.

"We should probably get cleaned up," Eve says, staring down at her blood-soaked dress. "If anyone sees us walking down the street like this, they might call the cops on us."

I'm not worried about human police. Most of them are in our pockets anyway, but still, I search around the small shed and rip into a box of paper towels. Pulling out a roll, I wind a bunch of sheets around my hand, tear off the end, and give the wad to her. She stares at it, confused for a second, but then gingerly takes it from me with a small smile.

"Thanks…"

I shrug. "I don't mind the blood on you. I actually prefer it."

She tries wiping herself down with the paper towels, but only succeeds in smearing the red across her breasts. My cock jumps in response, remembering just how tantalizing they felt in my hands.

This time, instead of giving in, I decide to pull up my zipper and tell myself I need to reel my thoughts and feelings about her back in.

I should probably be disgusted with myself for giving into such primal human urges, but right now, I don't care. Fucking Eve was as intoxicating as ending the Russian scumbag's life. Torturing and killing him together had been icing on the cake. She was quite a sight to behold, too. A thing of beauty.

She may try to act like she's repulsed by what I do, what I am, but she craves the darkness just like I do. The desire for destruction is in her veins.

Grunting in frustration, Eve throws the bloody paper towels and examines her nails, finding more blood underneath them.

"What I need is a shower," she says. "Kat's Kradle is only a few blocks from here. I can pop in and use the one behind the stage. Maybe see if Kat's there, or any of the other girls, too."

Immediately, I want to say no. The word hovers on my tongue, but when I look over at her, she's staring at me with hope in her eyes, and I have a sneaking suspicion that she's been wanting to find a way to visit her old job for some time. This chance just so happened to fall into her lap.

Maybe it's the high from the kill still fresh on my mind. Fuck, maybe it's the sex, I don't know, but I'm nodding before I realize what I've agreed to, or think about what Dracon might do if he finds out.

But it wins me a squeal of delight and a quick kiss on

the lips from Eve, and that's enough to stun me dumb for a few seconds.

I guess she's really missed her old life.

And, for some reason, I want to give her everything she desires. Which pisses me off. Being beholden to a woman? It's definitely gotta be the sex. That's how I found myself escorting the sexy little blonde down the street to the club where she used to dance.

"It's been so long since I've seen Kat," Eve says when I tune back in. She begins to tuck those delicious breasts back into her dress's top, and I frown, instantly missing them. "I hope she's doing okay."

"You give a shit what's going on with this human?" I ask, but I regret it the moment the words leave my mouth.

Eve scoffs, flipping her hair over her shoulder. "I see that the sex has really mellowed you out, Knox. And yes. I give a big shit about her, because Kat is like the mother I've always wanted and never had. She was there for me when I needed someone; she took me in when I was on the streets, and that counts for something."

She twists her dress back into place and adjusts her thin straps. Stepping over the dead man like he's no more than trash, she throws open the shed door and marches outside.

"You coming?" she calls over her shoulder.

I guess I am.

With one last glance at the body, I draw in a deep breath, feeling his soul's energy rattling inside my body, and stroll out after her.

Dracon's probably not going to like this, especially

when the entire reason I had to drag Eve on this excursion in the first place was because I was supposed to pick up money from one of our arms dealers, Jericho, behind Leah's clothing store. I was already late for the transaction and now we had to go the opposite way to get to Eve's old job.

No, Dracon wasn't going to like this at all.

The walk to the club is a short one, only a few blocks down, like Eve said. It's not open, but when Eve leads me to the back door, we find it broken and hanging partly open on its hinges.

"Dracon did that," she says in a low tone. "He had to kick it in when the Spades started shooting at us so we could take cover."

I nod. I would've done the same thing.

As she goes to reach for the handle, I take hold of it first and pull. The metal creaks and groans loudly, and when I get the thing open completely, the entire door pops off the top hinge completely and hangs unusable.

This place has definitely seen better days.

The moment we step inside I'm hit with a swell of human emotions. The place reeks of lust, greed, anger, and jealousy. It seems to seep from the walls around us.

Kat's Kradle is a sinner's heaven.

I love it.

I love it on principle.

"Kat? Demi? Mercy?" Eve bites her lower lip as she walks through the halls, calling out for her friends. "Hello! Anyone? Mack? Are you here?"

"Who's there?" The shaky reply comes from the front of the place, and I have no choice but to follow

Eve as she navigates through the back rooms and halls to the stage area.

Once we enter the large main area, we find the older witch—from the fight with Franco and Aris—and the owner of the club, Kat. She's sweeping around the tables, moving slow, and looking as worn down as she did the night we dropped her off with Eve's friend.

Kat looks up and squints our way. It takes her way too long to recognize Eve. Or me, which makes her flinch when she does, but that doesn't stop her from dropping the broom and shuffling over to us.

Eve meets her halfway and wraps her arms around her small frame.

"Oh my god!" Her eyes are round like she's just seen a ghost. "What are you doing here?"

My stomach flips at the sight; Eve, shaking, with her head buried in Kat's shoulder, both women clutching at the other, like they thought the other one was dead. It's strange to witness such affection this close up. The touchy, heart-melting kind.

Uncomfortable, I shrink back, keeping to the shadows. I could leave, and I'll admit, the idea does cross my mind briefly, but I stay put. No matter what, I can't take my eyes off Eve, entranced by the way she pulls back from Kat and rambles off answers to the witch's rapid-fire questions.

"Why are you covered in blood?"

"Did something else happen?"

"Are you okay?"

"Did he do it to you?"

Eve replies to all of them easily, but I'm not listening anymore. My gaze is on her lips, the way they move over each other and how her tongue dances as she talks. The way her chest moves up and down with each breath. The way she fiddles with her hands when she's nervous…

I'm transfixed by her. Maybe even more so than when we'd first met.

My cell buzzes in my pocket, shaking me from my trance. Yanking it out of my pocket, I find it's a text.

From Cassius.

Shit.

I guess it's better than Dracon but, as expected, he's wondering where the fuck we are and why I'm late picking up our money.

Still not well trained in how these cellphones work, I fumble with the small buttons to get out the message I need well enough—that I'm busy and where he can come meet us. It's riddled with mistakes, but he'll be able to make out what I'm trying to say anyway. He's known me long enough. Then I flip the phone to silent and tuck it back into my pants.

That's when I take in the room. Really take it in.

"What happened?" I ask out loud.

The sound of my voice has the two of them jumping in surprise. Eve's gaze sweeps across the destruction, noticing it for the first time, too. The place is a wreck, most of the tables broken into pieces, and half the chairs reduced to sawdust. Even the pole on the stage has been damaged. Something smashed right through the middle of it and left one piece dangling from the ceiling with the other jutting out of the wreckage like a broken bone.

"We're all fine. Okay? Everyone made it out," Kat assures Eve, and tries to offer her a small smile. "The night the Black Spades grabbed me, I put up a bit of a fight."

Eve shakes her head with a wavering smile. "Of course, you did, Kat. I mean, Christ, it looks like a tornado tore through the place."

The older witch must be pretty powerful to do this much damage to nab her. She's lucky her finger is all they took.

When Eve glances over to me, meeting my gaze, I know she's thinking the same thing.

"Demi and a few other of the girls are up stairs, helping me clear out the rooms. It shouldn't take too long to get things sorted," Kat goes on. "We're going to be closed up for a bit, I'm afraid. At least until I can get this place fixed up."

"What? No retirement?" Eve jokes, but Kat waves her hand dismissively.

"Retirement? Me? Nah. You know that if I stop moving my heart will stop, too. I'll just keel over."

The two women share another uneasy laugh before Eve's gaze travels over the room again and a frown transforms her face.

She rocks back on her heels. "Where are the rest of the girls? Are they still staying upstairs?"

"I have them at the Fairmont up the street for now. Some went home to their families. It's just not safe here right now. As much as I miss them, I can't risk it." I can tell Kat's a tough-as-nails, take-no-prisoners kind of businesswoman who refuses to let something like this stop her. A little hiccup in her world, even if it means financial ruin. She'll pick herself up and keep going, because she has people who depend on her.

"And before you ask. Yes, I'm still at Demi's for now. But I contacted my sister in Georgia, and she's going to let me stay there for a while so I can get out of her hair."

"Georgia?" Eve's voice rises. "But that's so far."

Kat's hands go to her hips, her hand with the missing finger still heavily bandaged. "What else am I supposed to do? I'll still be up here on weekends to get shit done. But, at the same time, I think I need a little break from…everything. Just a small one."

"I guess you're right," Eve says with a dark chuckle.

The chuckle does nothing to hide what's really going on inside her head, and a part of me loathes that I know it, that I'm close enough to Eve to realize what she's thinking. She sees this as her fault.

A low whistle rips through the space and I whirl to see Cassius cutting a path through the destruction. And dammit, but something inside of Eve softens at the sight of him.

"Cassius? What are you doing here?" she asks.

"Just couldn't stay away, sweetness," he replies with a wink. I notice Kat growing more nervous by the second at his sudden appearance. Too many members of the Kings of Eden in her space for her liking, I'm guessing.

"Thanks for meeting us here," I say to him. He reaches to clasp my arm in some man-like embrace, but

I dodge it, like I usually do. He knows I'm not a fan of touching.

Or of stupid human gestures.

Smooth as a cat, he pretends to be adjusting his coat instead to cover up my rejection. "Yeah, well, your text confused the shit out of me, so instead of facing Dracon's wrath, I decided to come down and find out what the hell you were smoking."

He smiles brightly at Kat. Creepily. And Eve touches her shoulder to walk her away from us and continue their conversation.

Now alone, Cassius turns to me and talks more freely.

"I'm confused as shit. Care to enlighten me?" he says. "You brought her here instead of meeting Jericho?"

"She's insistent when she wants to be."

His brows pinch. "But you listened to her."

"Like I said," I repeat. "She's insistent. She wanted to see her friend, so what's the harm?"

His gaze rakes over me like a physical presence I can actually feel on my skin. "And you're covered in blood?"

"When am I not?"

"True, but both of you? Did you run into trouble?"

"It was a minor thing. A nuisance really. We were followed by a Russian, but I took care of him," I reply.

A quick glance at Eve and Kat as they continue to talk in hushed whispers across the room, and then he shoots me a lopsided smile like he knows a secret I don't.

It's unsettling.

"What?" I ask.

"Something is different here…" he says. "Something with you and Eve."

"I don't know what the fuck you're talking about." I shake my head. "Nothing's different, Cassius. Not a goddamn thing. Fuck off."

He digs his finger into my side. "Or do you mean… Fuck *on*?"

"What the fuck is that supposed to me?" Is he speaking in tongues, or is that another living saying that I'm unfamiliar with?

"You did something. *Something* that's maybe more naughty than nice? Hmm?"

I only stare at him, but when his eyebrows shoot toward his hairline, I know he's figured it out. "Holy shit, you did! You finally did it! You fucked her."

"Shut your fucking mouth," I warn with a glare.

"Oh, wow, Dracon is going to have some words with you about that. I can't believe you actually went against everything you said, and you took her. She's sweet, isn't she?"

I know he's teasing me, like he usually does. Trying to get under my skin like a parasite, but that doesn't make listening to the truth of what I've done any easier. Maybe I'm not as strong as I thought. Not when it comes to Eve.

Cassius leans closer to me. "Did she blow you so good that she was able to convince you to come all the way over here?"

I'm struggling to keep my face devoid of emotion when I reply, "I just didn't see the harm in giving her this little thing."

"Sure. I see the way she's smiling, just like I see the way you're trying desperately to keep those walls high," he continues.

Cassius falls silent when one of the other girls comes into the main room—this one with a high ponytail and yoga pants. The moment the woman recognizes Eve, she erupts into a squeal so loud one of my eardrums nearly bursts.

"So, this is what she used to do," Cassius says in an undertone. "Her stage and her shining moments."

We've known our little dove used to dance for money for a living, and somehow it really brings the point home, looking around the ruined main room of Kat's Kradle now. Eve had a life before us. A life we've taken away from her when we claimed her for our own.

And yeah, I actually like seeing her have this sweet moment with her girls. I like seeing how something inside of her unwinds being back here, even with the place looking like a disaster zone.

"We're going to have to do something," I tell Cassius.

He turns to stare at me, though it means he has to look away from Eve. "Like what?"

"I don't fucking know." I shift awkwardly. "Something to help."

"Something to rebuild," he fills in.

"Yeah."

"I agree. This isn't cool."

I've nearly forgotten all about that shower Eve wanted, and she must have, too. My high is slowly fading away and is being replaced by an even worse sensation: responsibility for someone outside of myself and the other Kings.

I'm not sure when this little human woman managed to wrap me around her finger. Probably long before I slid my cock into her, if I'm being honest. Yet, things *have* changed, or at least started to shift between us. And I pray to whoever is out there listening that the change won't get any of us killed.

CHAPTER FOURTEEN

DRACON

The stench of death assaults my nostrils the moment I step out onto the balcony, where the last remnants of sunlight paint the horizon in oranges and reds.

A snap of power also zips up my spine, telling me I'm dealing with a very powerful supernatural near our home. I stiffen, knowing immediately what I'm dealing with.

Fucking vampire. When their bodies are reanimated, there's a taste of necromancy that has long been associated with the creation of vampires, and that's what I sense crawling over my skin.

The creature had some balls coming here, on my territory. The last time a vamp stepped foot into the Tower, the rogue bastard left in pieces in several body bags and ended up dumped in the river.

I sniff the air, lifting my head to where it originates. Looking toward the rooftop, I see no sign of anyone.

Doesn't mean they're not there. Vamps are the masters of concealment.

I flash back on my meeting with Alec in the alleyway the other night and wonder if it's him. Though what I smell seems more powerful.

Turning back inside, I march for the elevator and jab the button to the roof. My thoughts fly to Eve and worry if she's in danger. She's in her room, Knox remains in his morgue, and who the hell knows where Cassius is. Most likely jerking off somewhere thinking about Eve. I've seen how quickly he gets hard the moment she walks into the room. The guy's losing himself around her.

I shake those thoughts away and focus on the task at hand as I step out of the elevator and onto the rooftop of the Tower.

Scanning the terrace, I immediately spot the dark figure sitting in the lawn chair overlooking the city. His back is to me, and he would have heard my arrival from the click of the elevator doors. But he doesn't turn, and I stride toward him.

I skirt around the pool and push my hands into my pockets as I stroll closer, my gaze fixed on the dangerous vampire on my rooftop. He sits with one leg crossed over the other, his polished shoes shining beneath the moon. He's dressed in tailored pants, a fitted button-up black shirt, and he's lounging like he's the fucking warlord of the world. My hackles raise.

"Marius. This is an unexpected visit," I say, my voice firm. He twists his head to greet me, his graying hair perfect, not a strand out of place. The man is suave, always looking unperturbed by anything, but I wouldn't expect anything else from the leader of the Lords of Night and Master Vampire of Andover.

As Alpha, the way you conduct yourself filters down to your followers. Act like a fucking psycho, and you'll lose control of them in a heartbeat. Trust comes from the appearance as having control over your shit, even if you don't.

"I have a favor to repay," he says, a grin in his eyes.

I step up to the outdoor seat across from him, knowing he watches every move I make. I sit, knees parted, arms by my side. I'm not in the mood for company. I rarely am, but one never turns away Marius.

He might not have become an immortal until later in life, unlike Alec, but at five hundred years old, he's a dangerous motherfucker who's climbed his way to the top of the largest vampire clan in the country. You don't do that by playing nice.

"And what favor is that?" I ask.

I don't ignore the fact that he's in my home uninvited—a silent warning and power play.

I stare at the master vampire as he drags his tongue over his lower lip, studying me. "I owe you a favor for alerting me of the rogue vampires in the city a few weeks ago. Then, the other night, you offered Alec information about the missing Black Spaces and Russians." He uncrosses his legs and leans forward, arms folded across his thighs. "So, I'll share intel from my scouts to show I am a fair man."

"And what information do you have?" Marius isn't

the sharing kind, and despite his words, he'd have his own motives for doing this.

"Everyone's talking about what Cassius did to Dimitri's car," he suddenly says, steering the conversation in a different direction. "They say he's fuming that you humiliated him in front of others, and he's on a rampage to get back at the Kings. As there are already a lot of players in this city, if Dimitri decides to bring an army to your doorstep, that will be *your* war to contain." His unspoken words are loud—let the war spill into his turf and he'll blame me.

"Of course," I growl back, clear he has no intention of being in the line of fire. "I take care of my own business and territory. That asswipe Dimitri is not going to make a dent in my business." I shift in my seat. "Is that your favor repaid?" I snort, well aware it's more of a confirmation that he won't lift a finger to fight on our side should the city burn down around us than anything else.

Clearing his throat, he gets to his feet and strides over to the edge of the building, staring down at the darkened city. Shadows seem to follow him and he easily blends amongst them. Marius is the monster of nightmares, and I've heard the stories of him stealing people from their homes when the *feed* takes him over, when he loses control. I've seen the aftermath myself, his signature scent on the scene with half a dozen people torn apart in minutes, totally drained of blood. There's a reason many fear the Lords.

"Franco's been spotted near the entry to the old

catacombs at the edge of town," Marius mutters, his deep voice breaking through my thoughts.

I jump to my feet and turn toward him, tense. "The fuckhead's gone underground?"

Anger runs through my veins, fury pummeling into me to tear apart Franco and Dimitri. The more I hear their names, the more determined I am to hunt them down. I don't hear the next words from Marius as my head throbs with the darkness of my thoughts.

The vampire twists to stare at me over his shoulder with a raised eyebrow. "I trust I have paid off my favor and you will take care of this mess," he states, finality in his tone, then turns away from me, his voice growing tired of the conversation.

Fuck, I'm tired of looking at his face.

One moment, he stands there, the next, there's only a trace of darkness sweeping up and over the edge of the building. He's gone just like that, merged into the night.

Snarling under my breath, I curl my hands into fists, not appreciating his underhanded warning while alluding to the fact that he was repaying me a favor. Despite dancing with the vampire, he told me where Franco was.

I turn and dart across the rooftop, ready to tear out the Black Spades' throat.

The time for sitting back and waiting is over. It's finally time these fuckers who mess with us are eliminated. Anyone gets in my way, and they're going down. First Franco and Dimitri, and if Marius gets in my face again, I'll fuck him up.

By the time I'm standing in a filthy backstreet with the city humming in the background, my pulse is an inferno. I click lock on my Lamborghini and push the keys into my pocket as I cross the cobblestone street.

This is the old part of Andover, where many homes remain abandoned, where the poor live, where the Black Spades rule. It never occurred to me that Franco the worm would slither into the underground catacombs, mostly because not many linger in this sector. Hundreds died during the great fire that tore through the city a long time ago. After that, the place was completely rebuilt, over the top of the dead and the bones of the old city. Some of the tunnels contain old homes and the remains of those who lost their lives, and I'd heard some homeless live down there.

I approach an arched, metal door that looks new compared to the filthy stone walls of the side-by-side old buildings. I grab hold of the metal chain keeping it locked and wrench it off. I toss it to the ground with a clang, then pull the door open.

Instantly, I'm hit with the heavy stench of freshly turned soil and piss. Darkness swallows everything. Using the light on my cell phone, I march through the narrow passages. The walls are covered in gaping holes and graffiti, the floor littered with trash and syringes.

A few rooms I pass have disgusting mattresses and blankets on the floor, where I assume squatters used to stay. Maybe they still do if there's another entrance. They are all empty now.

I keep following the passage, taking the steps to the basement, needing to get to the catacombs. I'd been here once before, a long time ago with Saxon when there were no locks, just an open passage.

But I shake those thoughts away, along with the ache burning in my chest.

Sniffing the air gives me nothing. No scent to follow, only the stuffy smell of dank earth. But I move forward regardless.

I don't know how long I search the tunnels underground, but I find nothing.

No Franco.

None of his Black Spades gang.

Not a fucking thing.

Had they abandoned the place? Marius isn't someone to lie. There's no reason for him to.

By the time I retrace my steps and head back outside, I make the decision to position some of our men in this sector of the city, especially around the entry until someone sees something. Until I track down that fucking bastard, Franco.

EVE

The night is silent, the hallway dark, and only the beating pulse of my heart thumps in my ears.

It's not my intention to be walking around in the dark in the Tower in the middle of the night, but my throat was parched and now, for some reason, instead of going back to my room, I find myself heading right for Cassius's.

Once upon a time, very little scared me. In hindsight, despite working in a strip club, I lived a very sheltered life. I believed what I did had nothing to do with the gangs and criminals in the city. As long as I kept away from them, I could continue living blissfully unaware.

And now look at me, I'm up to my eyeballs in death threats. That would make any girl paranoid. These days, darkness holds a very different fear, especially after my recent kidnapping by Dimitri.

I've lost my freedom, but I'm not foolish enough to lose my life, so whatever it takes to live with the Kings, I'll do it. Even sneak into their bedroom in the middle of the night to ease away the shivers over my skin.

Cassius's door sits slightly ajar, and I push it open just enough for me to stick my head inside.

It's dark, the air stifling. The bed's empty, the sheet bunched up on one side, as if someone shoved it away when they got out of bed quickly.

"Come in, Eve," Cassius says from across the room, and my gaze follows the voice to find him standing by the window with his back to me.

Strong, round shoulders glow under the silvery hue of the moonlight pouring through the window. Shadows hide the bottom half of his body, but I can already tell he's not wearing anything.

"Can't sleep?" I ask, padding toward him on bare feet across the floorboards.

"I miss the heat," he tells me. "No matter how much I warm up my room, I can never seem to achieve that perfect scorching burning that calms me."

"Feels pretty toasty in here already," I say, pausing by his side and staring out the window to see what's caught his attention. All I spot are two pigeons grooming themselves on the windowsill. "Do you miss Hell?"

He shrugs, staring down at the critters making a mess of feathers everywhere. "Sometimes it keeps me awake all night. So I stare outside, waiting for something to wash the memories away. I guess that's you tonight."

Silence envelopes us.

When I turn to look up at him, there's a fiery glint in his eyes, the look triggering my instinct to recoil from him. I lift my hands and cross them over my chest, suddenly aware of how thin the fabric of my pajama top is and how stiff my nipples are.

He blinks a few times, and I'm staring into the deep blue eyes I am familiar with.

"I-I was thirsty and couldn't sleep either," I admit, feeling awkward and saying the first thing that came to mind.

A grin curls on his lips, and there's the Cassius I know. The King who hides behind jokes and flirting, except something ominous had been on his mind before I arrived, something he doesn't want to talk about.

"Come to bed with me," he says, then takes my hand, and I don't resist. After all, I willingly came to his room. Even if I couldn't articulate to myself the reason for it, I knew it had to do with needing company. Cassius has always been the most approachable, and he makes me laugh more often than not.

Hand in hand with a naked demon, I follow him to

bed, but I pull my hand from his when I glanced down. My eyes went wide at this demon's spectacular form. The guy was an Adonis. Cut muscles, angles, and valleys across his solid chest and stomach, biceps big enough to bench press this entire building. Then I let my gaze dip to his erection.

Of course, he's already thick and hard. And we hadn't even teased each other. I inhale deeply, well aware of what I'm getting myself into.

He shuffles over in bed and rolls onto his side, tapping the mattress in front of him. "Get your cute ass over here."

I lean forward but he makes a tsking sound. He blinks those long lashes at me. "I have only one rule in my bed. No clothes."

I arch an eyebrow. "Then I can just as easily go back to my room."

"Go for it. Remember, you came here, not the other way around. Plus, I'm not saying I'm going to fuck you, just that no one can get into my bed with clothes."

He's tapping the mattress in front of him again, smirking, and I want to tear that smug look off his face. But, he's got a point. I did come to him for company, because the darkness in my room unsettles me tonight.

To avoid giving him the upper hand, I reach over and snatch the bedsheet, then, by some sheer level of magic, I strip and wrap myself in the bedsheet without flashing him. Now, I resemble a Greek goddess in a toga and am rather proud of myself.

"I said no clothes," he mutters, staring at me with a delicious grin curling his mouth.

"I'm not wearing any, just your bed sheet which was on your bed anyway. Technically, I'm not breaking your rules." I throw myself onto the bed and bounce on the mattress, poking my tongue out at him.

"You're asking for trouble," he purrs, large arms grabbing me around the middle and dragging me toward him. He rolls me onto my side so I'm looking away from him before he locks an arm around my hips. He pulls my body roughly against his, my ass cradled against his erection, his grip hardening.

"Hey." I fight against him. "Not so rough."

"Don't worry, I know what you want," he whispers in my ear, his hot breath dancing across my cheek. It sends beautiful shivers down my back, and I arch against him, my body reacting so quickly from his breath alone.

"Yeah?" I gasp the word. "And what's that?"

"To be held while you tell me what's on your mind."

I laugh out loud, failing miserably at unlocking his arms from around my body. He's got his leg over mine, pinning me in place.

"You've been watching too many TV dramas."

"Am I wrong?" he asks, his breath on my ear again, and he knows perfectly well the influence he has on me. "So, tell me, why are you sneaking into my room in the middle of the night? I can guess, if you'd prefer."

"Go for it. Should be fun," I answer, attempting to shuffle away from him and failing miserably. I resign myself to the fact that I'm stuck for now. So, with my head resting on a huge bicep, and the heat of his body blanketing me, I settle down.

"I'm thinking of two possibilities. First, is the obvious one. You're horny and can't get enough of demon cock."

I burst out laughing at how cocky he sounds. "It's obvious that I'm horny, is it? You are delusional."

He breathes heavily once more, and his hand around my middle glides upward, ever so gently brushing across my nipples.

My heart races and I draw in a raspy breath as that simple touch has me tingling all over.

"Am I getting close?" he whispers, igniting the heat inside me so fast, I want to scream.

I bat at his arm, but he snatches it and locks it against my side with his. "Look at how erect your nipples are, how much they want me to suck on them." He grinds his cock against my ass, and goddamn him, but I crave him. The bastard knows it, and he has no problem pointing out the obvious.

"Just say the word, Eve, and I'll unwrap you with my teeth, then I'll only touch you with my tongue. I'll lap up the juices between your legs, I'll make you wrap your legs around my head so I tongue fuck you until you scream for my cock. Then, when you're ready, I'll fuck you like a beast."

I tremble against him, hating how easily his words affected me.

"Do you know how hard it is to be around you and keep my dick in my pants?" he whispers in my ear. "All I can think about is pushing my cock into your pussy. I want it so bad that it makes me obsess over you. I want to be the ruthless monster in your life, to have you wake up with my name on your lips as you orgasm from the fantasies I plant in your mind. I want to break you, Eve, to show you all the ways I can bring you pleasure, then piece you back together like the goddess you are."

My pulse is racing, a buzz running over my nerves, silk already coating my pussy. I am holding onto his arm, desperate to catch my breath.

Damn him. This is exactly what he wanted, isn't it?

"A-And what is your second guess?" My voice comes out raspy and my cheeks are on fire. I keep my thighs pressed tight together, knowing that one touch from him down there, and I'll give him anything he wants.

He doesn't respond right away. Instead, his fingers dig into my hip, his other hand wrapped around my shoulder, holding me so tightly I fear he's trying to pull me into him. Yet, I don't move. Not while my heart thunders in my ears and all I can picture is Cassius taking the peak of my breasts into his mouth. How warm he'd feel, how his wicked tongue would flick my nipples.

I'm teasing myself, and as much as I toyed with the notion of sliding my hand behind me and cupping his cock, I also know after that there'd be no turning back.

"The dark scares you," he says with a clear throat.

Those simple words give me a pause.

Before I can respond, he continues. "What you've been through lately is fucked up, so it makes sense that being alone in your room in the dark, paranoia would play havoc with your mind."

"Interesting," I say.

"And you know what I think?" he continues, even if I

can't seem to stop focusing on how hard his body is pressed up against me, how his cock hasn't gone down.

"What's that?"

"You came here to not be alone in the dark, but unknowingly, you came to sit on my cock."

I burst out laughing that time, unable to hold it back. "Is it always about sex with you?"

"And it's not for you?"

I shrug, and well, I couldn't exactly deny it, either.

"You want to know something?" he asks, his voice more sincere this time, like he's about to share his wisdom.

"Sure," I reply.

"After the whole ordeal, ending up abandoned on Earth, it took me a long time to sleep without night-mares. The only way I was able to was to sleep to music. It's ridiculous, but I learned that it helped me focus on the tunes and not the fucked-up shit in my head. So, what you need is a distraction from your mind demons."

Mulling over his words, I came to the conclusion that he wasn't spinning shit for a change. "That actually makes sense."

"Don't sound too surprised." He nibbles on my ear, awakening the blaze deep in my core. "How about this? You're welcome to come sleep in my bed any night. You just need a distraction from your thoughts, right? Even if you don't want sex, we can just lie here. But no clothes or bed sheets next time."

For a fraction of a second, I considered how each time I came to him, we'd probably end up having sex, but I also appreciated his offer. "Thank you. That means a lot. I'll take you up on it, starting tonight."

I shuffle slightly to get myself comfortable and breathe easier.

"Oh, so you're going to get some sleep now?" he asks, slowly rocking his erection against my ass cheeks.

"Yep. Good night, Cassius." I breathe deep, well aware of what a tease I am, but technically the only person doing the teasing tonight was him, not me.

I don't recall how long I lay pressed up against him, but as my eyelids grow heavier, I let them fall and I sink into my dreams.

A delicious tingle spreads between my legs, the kind that intensifies, that fills me with filthy thoughts. Where my hips rock out of instinct and desire builds within me.

It's delicious, the sensation heightening, and right now I can't tell if I'm half-asleep or having the most incredibly erotic dream.

It's only when I hear a groan that I freeze, then jerk my head up, my eyes snapping open.

I look down at my naked body to where Cassius sticks his head up from between my legs, his lips and chin glistening with my cum, and he grins. "Morning, gorgeous."

My breath catches in my throat as I try to say his name, but as he pushes a finger into me, all I manage is a moan.

"Cassius," I finally purr. "What the hell?" Never in my wildest dreams have I expected to wake up with a gorgeous demon between my legs, sucking on my...I moan louder as he flicks my clit.

"Yes, my gorgeous. I have to say, you are ridiculously beautiful, spread like this, and your pussy is like nectar." Then he goes to town on me without warning, eating me enthusiastically, my pulse thundering.

"Oh, fuck," I cry out, my head falling back onto the pillow as I fist the bedsheets. He's pressing his tongue into me, his nose rubbing my clit, and I'm about to erupt. I rub my pussy against his face and he's growling, loving it.

For a moment, I'm transfixed on the ceiling, listening to the devious licking sounds he makes, loving how he pushes my legs wider, how he's practically eating all of me with his huge mouth.

This demon should come with a warning label. Side effects may induce multiple orgasms. Always carry a spare pair of panties.

Hungry, needy lust consumes me. I'm moving my hips back and forth, my moans growing louder, and there's no holding back how much he's rocking my world.

The orgasm comes at me fast. It knocks into me hard, owns me, consumes me. I scream while my demon's tongue fucks me, taking everything I have and lapping it up. A flurry of shivers cover me while he pushes his tongue in and out of me. Every sensation has me moaning louder.

I have no idea how long we're locked this way, his

face planted between my legs, but the sounds he makes. Fuck me, I might just orgasm from the guttural growls alone. Having a man make such noises from eating your pussy is euphoric. It gives a girl unimaginable confidence.

When he finally releases me, he stares at me with such savagery that I tremble with need. His eyes darken, and I'm not sure if his demon is coming forward, but I don't care.

"Are you going to be a good girl for me?" This huge man crawls over me like a monster. He's massive and I suddenly feel so tiny beneath him, especially when I glance down between us and stare at how well he's hung. I remember the first time we fucked and his size was surprising.

But I'm ready, and I lay for him spread, dripping wet, moaning for more.

"Yes," I finally respond. "I'm always a good girl."

"Good, because I'm hungry, Eve, and I can't promise I'll be gentle. But I promise you that you will scream for me."

An excited shiver races down my spine and curls over the nerves of my pussy, leaving me covered in tingles.

There's no stopping this even if I wanted to, but of course I don't. "Come over here, my big bad demon," I purr, teasing him, reaching for his shoulders to draw him near. Tilting my hips up, I curl my legs around his hips

He presses the head of his cock into me and I gasp, remembering very well how big he felt inside me.

"Relax, gorgeous," he growls, the muscles in his neck tensing, as I know he's barely holding back. He's got his hands planted on either side of my shoulder, trapping my body with his as he pushes into me. I wriggle to position myself for as much comfort as possible, ready for this wild ride.

"I'm going to fuck you now, Eve, and I'm going to fill your tight little hole with all my cum." He grins, clearly a fantasy he'd been having. But there's no time for me to respond, not when he pushes into me, spreading me, stretching me. And, *oh, fuck*. I stiffen, my fingers digging into his shoulder as he goes deeper and deeper while I'm stretched wider.

He calms me with soothing sounds, while with each stroke he pushes father into me until I feel the heat of his balls against my ass.

His eyes are fluttering back. "Hell, you're strangling my cock, and I fucking love it."

Lowering himself closer, he captures my mouth with his as he pulls out and drives back into me. His kiss is full of passion and hunger.

I moan and writhe underneath him as he slowly drags his mouth down my chin, my neck, and then aggressively sucks my nipple into mouth. He tugs on it, flicking it, while his hips pick up tempo.

I hold onto him, my body swimming in arousal, riding the sharp edge Cassius is pushing me toward.

Crying out from how hard he bites into my breast only escalates the lust licking my insides. He pulls back suddenly, sitting on his knees between my legs. Large hands grab my hips and lift me closer to him then take hold of my ankles. He spreads them.

"If you could only see the scene from here, you'd come instantly. How beautifully your pussy stretches open to take me, how you suck on my cock."

I attempt to respond, but he drives into me so hard that I scream instead. His hard cock plunges into me, and I have no control of my body. He claims me, owns me, and does as he pleases.

I tilt my head back, arching my back the faster he takes me, my nipples erect, knowing I am close. I feel it building inside me from the fiery friction of his cock.

"Eyes on me, gorgeous. I want to see your face when I fuck you. I'm going to fuck you all day."

I shudder beneath him, and my body seems to have other plans. "I can't hold back anymore," I moan.

Drawing in a deep breath, I already feel the orgasm pressing forward and readying to drag me under its spell.

He pumps into me, growling, his eyes fiery. "Come for me then, because I will be sure to give you at least three more orgasms today."

His confession has me gasping with shock, but I forget that as he fucks me savagely.

"Cassius...Cas..." I scream, my body convulsing as the orgasm plunges through me. It tears my insides in the most beautiful way.

Cassius howls. "Yes, fucking squeeze my cock, milk me, Eve, milk me!"

If I wasn't drowning under the most incredible orgasm, I might have told him to keep it the hell down, because I'm pretty sure the whole city heard him screaming for me to milk him. That's when I sense him pulsing inside me, the warmth of his seed flooding with me.

He pauses, then falls down over me, hands on the mattress as his eyes darken. This delicious demon shudders as he pumps me full. I'm riding my own wave of exhilaration, and with how hard my heart is banging, I'm certain she's close to giving out.

I close my eyes and enjoy the sensations humming over my body, adoring how incredible Cassius feels buried deep inside me, and most of all, I love how he peppers my face with kisses like I'm someone special.

CHAPTER FIFTEEN

EVE

I can't stop thinking about what happened back at Kat's Kradle. Not just seeing the girls, although I'd been itching to get back there for way longer than I wanted to admit to myself. But the decimated main room. The destruction that left the woman I cared about with broken pipes and more damage than she'd be able to bounce back from. Plus, Kat, in the center of it all, with a damn push broom like that was somehow going to make a difference.

I need to do something to help her, but my hands are tied. I'm lucky Knox let me go to the club in the first place. And seeing Cassius there...but neither one of them dragged me away. Not until I'd gotten a chance to catch up with Kat and Demi. Even then, they'd been reluctant to leave, despite this being a side trip.

I'm grateful for it, which is something I never thought I'd say about the Kings in any capacity.

Sighing, I flip over to my side, snuggling deeper into the softness of the mattress. The sun outside is completely unbothered by what happened the day before, and I'm so lost in my thoughts I don't even want to get up.

I've gotta do something. Something to help, although there isn't shit I can do for Kat. I don't have the means to help her rebuild, and I doubt the guys will let me out of their sight long enough to physically *do* anything.

Oddly enough, my thoughts shift to Saxon, the glue that had held the Kings of Eden together, the one they struggle to forge ahead without. Dracon would hate my help even when he needs it. My friends are the most important things in the world to me. If Saxon was important to Dracon, who doesn't seem to care about anyone, then learning more about him through Dracon's memory might be what I need to get through. To start carving away at the ice around their hearts.

I'm not the type of person to sit around with my thumb up my ass when it's in my power to do something.

To help.

And these men? *Dracon?* They need help.

Forcing myself out of bed, I dress and toss my hair up in a messy bun. Saxon, Dracon's best friend and wolf shifter. They'd known each other for like a century before Saxon died. Now the Kings are all at each other's throats.

I'd found the room by accident the first time, wandering through the halls and lost in my own thoughts. This time, and despite the cameras watching my progress, I head there on purpose.

For answers.

Finding out more about the guy will be a two-birds, one-stone kind of deal—a distraction from the tumbling thoughts creating chaos inside my brain, and an outlet for my need to do something, anything, to ease tensions.

Despite my exhaustion, and the ache between my legs from being with Knox yesterday and Cassius this morning, I climb the stairs, my fingers trailing along the ornate railing. Another long hallway greets me at the top.

The quarters of the Kings.

The gym, more bedrooms, a conference room, and Dracon's room. I pass them all and head toward the last door, past the library with the dazzling view of the city and mountains in the distance.

I keep meaning to spend more time in the library. Yeah, right. Maybe in another life. The next door over opens to the same enormous bed draped in black sheets. Clothes still litter the floor and I stare at the dangling handcuffs with an emotional distance I didn't possess the last time I came here.

Everything is untouched, still in its place. Dracon and the others must not be able to bring themselves to touch a single item.

Saxon liked kink. I knew that much about him, not only from the handcuffs, but because of the other Kings. They all have similar tastes when it comes to sex.

Not that I mind.

I like it.

Knowing I shouldn't be here, and what Dracon will

likely do to me if he finds me in this room again, I step purposely over the threshold. There are no books whatsoever here, despite the proximity to the library. Aside from the clothing and toiletries, there isn't much about Saxon I can see from a cursory glance around the messy space. The clothes in the closet—hanging half-on and half-off the hangers—and the view out the windows speaks to a person who lived life on the edge, always in a hurry. Someone who wouldn't want to waste a single moment focusing on anything unpleasant.

What was it about Saxon that did so much for the others? What about his personality made it a more cohesive ecosystem when the four of them had been together?

And what happened to shake the others loose once he died?

They were all zip-lipped. They'd rather slit my throat then give me an inch, although I'd gotten several glorious inches from each of them now.

Conversation wise?

Emotional wise?

They wouldn't let me in.

I step further into the room, closing my eyes and drawing in a deep inhale. The damp smell of mold wouldn't permeate this space even with its occupant gone. Dracon would make sure of that, and although it wasn't exactly clean, the dry scent of dust melded with the rich and musky undertone of the man. The shifter.

"What are you doing?"

I try not to jump at the sound of Dracon's voice, filled with ice and directly next to my ear.

"What does it look like I'm doing?" I ask instead. "I'm communing with the spirits."

"You better fucking not be. Get out of here right now."

The fury in his voice is enough to have my heart jerking in my chest and beating loudly enough for both of us to hear. Instead of backing down, the way I automatically want to, I straighten my spine.

"No."

My eyes pop open when he grabs my wrist, whirling me around to face him. His pupils glow red and I swear smoke curls from his nostrils and ears.

"No?" he repeats with dangerous softness.

I draw in a deep breath, holding it for several tense seconds before exhaling roughly. "No," I say again. "I'm not going to leave. Not even if you're super angry with me for being here in the first place."

He tightens his hold on me, his fingers bite against my skin with bruising strength. "Make no mistake, Eve. I'm furious. I told you not to come here again, and not only have you come back, you're acting like you have every fucking right to be here."

"I just want to know—" I start.

"What?" he snaps.

"I want to know about him. And about you."

"It's none of your business!" His voice raises until he's roaring in my face and I want to flinch. I want to curl up in a tiny ball to withstand his ire. "Can't you fucking see? I'm trying to literally preserve this room the way it was before he died. And when you come in here, mucking around, breathing—"

"Breathing?" I interrupt.

"Then you risk wrecking it. That's why it hasn't changed at all since the day he passed."

"I'm sorry." I don't dare try to take my hand back from him. "I wasn't going to disturb anything."

Dracon's gaze bores into mine until I feel it pierce right through me and out the other side.

"I can't take that chance. Get back to your room."

At the risk of sounding like a petulant toddler, I adjusted my stance and set him with a hard gaze of my own. "No. I want answers, Dracon, and I think that I can find them here."

A hint of amusement trickles into his expression. "Answers to what, Eve? Any answers you hope to find here are for questions you have no business asking."

"I'm not going to leave until I find out more about this place. And about you. I want to know how you all tick, and I think Saxon will help me better understand you."

Dracon sighs, dropping my hand suddenly enough that I wince. "When are you going to get it? You are not free to do what you want, to go wherever you please. You're a prisoner."

A sex slave, sure, I get that, although I will never tell any of the guys that I like the sex. "As long as I'm here with the three of you, then it's my business what goes on," I reply harshly.

At least he isn't screaming at me anymore. A little of the fight seems to have left him, although he's still staring at me like it will physically hurt him to see any part of this room. Any part of the perfectly preserved memory of the friend he'd lost.

"It's not going to change anything, Eve."

Taking a risk, and knowing it might literally bite me in the ass, I step up to him. I get in Dracon's face, though not with any kind of antagonization. Instead, I place my palm on his cheek, arm tingling with the return of blood to the area.

"Things need to change," I say. "Keeping this room as it was when he died is not going to somehow help the three of you together. It's not going to improve the relations between you."

"That's not why I keep it," he growls.

"You're not trying to preserve his memory?"

He's not knocking my hand away, either. He's not moving a muscle. It's as though this big, bad shifter has turned into a statue rather than a living and breathing man. Like my touch has paralyzed him.

Or maybe it's being back in this space again.

"Is it so wrong if I want to?" he finally asks.

I shake my head before saying, "Not at all. But your memories are your own. They're inside your head and your heart. I'm just trying to figure out a way to help you."

He narrows his eyes. "I don't want your help."

"Then why do you keep me?"

"I'd think it obvious." His voice drops into a purr. "Your talents lie between your legs."

"So you've said. But if we're going to make this work, the *four* of us, then you've got to let me in a little bit. There are things I can do that will make life easier for you."

"And you believe that fucking you does not accomplish that?"

"Maybe it would help me a little bit if you let me in," I admitted. "Not that you give two shits about my mental health and wellbeing, but I think this might be a good step. For all of us."

He's silent for a long moment before smacking his palm over my hand. Seconds later, his fingers link with mine, squeezing softly before breaking my hold on him. "Okay. It might be time that we pack some of this stuff up. And it might go easier if you stay," Dracon replies.

I duck my head to hide my smile from him. This small victory, as minuscule as it seems in the grand scheme of life, means a lot to me. "I'll help you."

CHAPTER SIXTEEN

KNOX

I woke up feeling like shit.

When I finally showered and managed to semi-compose myself, I left my morgue to join the others upstairs. Mostly because I'm stir-crazy and if I keep pacing, I'll wear a hole to the basement.

Thing is, everyone's still asleep. Fair enough, considering it's barely six in the morning. When all hell breaks loose, I have no problems funneling my energy into something more constructive. It's when my most creative torture ideas come to life.

Except right now, my muse is a desert. I'm dried up, and it's fucking pissing me off. It's all Aris's fault.

Then there's Eve, the girl I should have eliminated. Instead, everything is messed up in my head over what is right and wrong.

I find myself standing outside Eve's room of all places, and yet I'm not walking away. Instead, I push down on the handle and enter. It's dim in here, and her sweet smell finds me immediately. Quick, silent steps take me across the room and I stand feet away from her bed, staring down at this beauty. Wild hair sits in a messy halo around her head on the pillow. She's on her side, one leg sticking out of the blanket, the rest of her tucked underneath it.

Her eyes are moving rapidly behind her closed eyelids, telling me she's in a deep dream state. Part of me wonders how she'd react if I climbed into bed with her. I want to find out, as I imagine she'd be fiery. And maybe that's what I need. An argument to get my creative juices flowing so I can find a fucker to torture and feel like my old self.

But the longer I stare at her, the more I can't bring myself to wake her up. My emotions are all twisted up when it comes to Eve. She's brought something out in me I never expected. And standing in her room, staring at her sleeping isn't helping me with my agitated state, so I compose myself and leave, shutting the door behind me.

Out on the balcony, the morning breeze is cool on my skin. The city sleeps, though down below, cars are already zipping down the road, and that's when something white catches my attention from the street corner.

I squint my eyes for a better look because even with perfect eyesight, I'm damn high up. There's someone standing down on the street corner in a white shirt and jeans staring up, directly my way.

And even from my vantage spot, I instantly know I'm staring at the fuckhead, Aris. I'd know him anywhere.

He's back, and lava boils in my veins.

The idiot is unresponsive to the honking cabs, to anything around him. He's in a frozen state, staring at our Tower, telling me he's still in his haze. And yet, he's drawn to us.

My heartbeat thunders, aching with the urgency to destroy him. Heaviness hit me like a tsunami, and I can't escape the ominous reminder of what Aris represents.

Death for all of us. And the fact he stands there, all spaced out, makes him vulnerable.

I turn abruptly and run for the elevator, rage pounding my head. The weight of the Mortem Blade at my belt brings me comfort; the time has come for me to do what I should have done a long time ago.

The elevator slides open, and I throw myself inside, slapping my hand on the ground-floor button.

I'm bouncing on my feet—and here I thought I'd lost my killing muse. When, all this time, I'd craved to destroy the only thing that came close to being my equal. Aris.

His death flares over my mind. It's only a matter of time until he'll return to his full force, so I need to stop wasting my time and eradicate him now. There's no shame in eliminating your enemy when they are down...that's the smarter decision.

And since when did I give a fuck about playing nice?

I shove myself out of the elevator as soon as it opens and cut across the hallways, finally escaping the Tower.

I'm out on the sidewalk, sucking in raspy breaths, and sprint to the corner, my hand on my blade, my fingers twitching to jab it right into Aris's heart.

At the intersection, I pause, staring across the road to where Aris had been.

But he's gone.

"Fuck no. Where the hell are you?" I grumble under my breath. "You're not going to get away from me this time. Not again." I sprint across the road, much to the annoyance of the oncoming drivers who honk at me. But I don't have time for pedestrian etiquette.

I have a monster to track and destroy. And if he was just here, then he hasn't gotten far. I charge down the side street, ready to hunt him down for as long as it fucking takes.

EVE

"Have you seen Knox?" I ask, flopping down on the couch next to Cassius because he's got a bowl of popcorn. Plus, I woke up with a strange feeling this morning that I sensed Knox's presence. I haven't seen him all day, and seeing how unpredictable he is, part of me is worried.

Cassius shrugs. "Hunting or killing would be my guess. Don't care right now, as he's in such a shitty state, he's going to just kill the mood."

"Yeah, and what mood is that?" I ask, grabbing some popcorn and stuffing it into my mouth. Oh, this tastes just like the one from the theaters. I take more from the bowl in Cassius's lap.

"Movie night," he states, smirking a bit too greedily.

I eye him, suddenly feeling like I'm missing a joke.

"You normally hold movie nights?" I ask. "Don't get me wrong, it's great, but just not something I ever pictured. Now I'm curious about your choice of movies. Thinking something graphic with blood and lots of sex. God, tell me we're not watching a porno."

He's laughing at me, but is also staring right into my soul, like maybe I'd guessed right. Seriously, if he pulls that crap on me, I'm throwing all this popcorn over his head.

After the shitty week I've been having, the constant stress, I want something to make me laugh.

Leaning back and taking the bowl into my lap, I tuck my legs under me and say, "Okay, hit me. I'm ready for anything you've got."

With a mischievous grin, Cassius gets to his feet and switches off the light, only the glow from the white screen on the television illuminating the room.

"Is Dracon joining us, too?" I ask.

"Doubt it. He's got a conference call or something." Cassius is fiddling with the TV, inserting something into the side that looks like a USB drive. So, we're not going to stream something?

Then he comes back to the couch and sits next to me, remote control in hand. He doesn't say a word, simply hits play. He takes the bowl of popcorn from me and sets it on the table behind the couch.

He shuffles close and wraps an arm around my waist, drawing me to practically sit on his lap.

The screen goes dark at first, then it suddenly flickers to white fuzzy lines across the screen horizontally, and the longer I stare at it, the more I'm convinced we're about to watch some black-market demon sex porn.

The screen starts flickering to a bad quality black-and-white screen, the view looking top down in a room with someone's bed. There's a girl in it, and I'm halfway through rolling my eyes hard at how predictable Cassius is, until—

My stomach goes cold.

I find myself staring at my own face on the screen.

My mouth falls open. What the hell?

It takes several seconds of my brain scrambling before I understand exactly what I'm staring at.

"Are you fucking kidding me?" I snap. "You're showing me the video of me in my bedroom?"

Cassius turns to face me, his grip tightening. "Keep watching. It's when you first arrived at our Tower and you thought you were so smart to get back at us."

He arches an eyebrow, and there's lust swimming in his eyes. I look back at the TV just as I slide my hand down my body and between my legs, showing the camera everything.

Already, I see Cassius's pants tenting, and I twist to him. "How many—"

"Shhh." He places a finger to my mouth. "This is the best part. Fuck me, Eve, but I can't tell you how many times I've jerked off to this scene."

The thing is, as much as my hackles are raised, I'm also slightly turned on thinking of the impact I've had on him. I've never been one to be shy of my body. Even being curvy, I embraced every inch of myself long ago, or I would have never succeeded at Kat's Kradle.

Having men melt for your body does things to boost your confidence. Besides, what I learned working at the club is that most men worship female bodies. They adore every size and shape we come in as most of the time they have tunnel vision. They are so fucking randy that they see only the things that turn them on. No cellulite, no love handles. Just how gorgeous we are.

It took me a while to get used to that.

If this gorgeous, Adonis of a demon is lusting over me playing with myself on the screen, then I'm not going to run away.

Hearing his rushed breathing and seeing how sensual I actually look sends a buzz down my spine and to the melting pot between my thighs.

"It's hot to see you getting off on this video of me," I say to him, lounging back. Though, he's still got his arm tightly wound around my waist, which makes sense. He had no intention of letting me go in case I got pissed over the screening.

Cassius suddenly flicks off the television and twists around to face me, licking his lips. Those enchanting eyes send me into my own spiral of desires. Maybe it's the fact that we're in the dark, or that, outside, the soft pitter-patter of rain hits the windows, but my pulse has kicked up a notch.

Hell. I'm already smitten with Cassius, and it seems every time we're alone, we end up all over each other.

"I was hoping you'd approve," he tells me, drawing me toward him.

His breath is on my face as he stares down at me, and I draw in a shallow breath, suddenly aware of his burning hot skin against me, his hand having already slipped under the elastic of my sweatpants.

In a heartbeat, he's got me up and straddling his lap. I gasp, mostly because of how easily he swings me around.

"It seems you know what you want," I reply with a small laugh.

"I'm extremely attracted to you, Eve. I don't play games. I wake up with you on my thoughts and my cock hard, and every time I see you, I just want you to climb me like a fucking tree. So, I'm not going to be apologetic for wanting you when I see the desire in your eyes...I smell it on you."

"I'm making a mental note that you're easy." I snort a laugh, then burst out louder that I actually made a snorting sound. Bless the dark for hiding my blushing cheeks.

"Honestly, I could sit here with you rubbing yourself against my cock all night, just watching you smile, listening to you. But it might be a lot more fun if we remove our clothes, then resume." His fingers trail back and forth across my lower back, his touch soft enough to send shivers across my body and there's something passionate about the way he touches me just enough to drive me crazy.

"I'm surprised that you haven't already torn my clothes off, considering how hard your cock is." I rock myself against his erection, using it as my personal fuck stick, rubbing myself right where it feels incredible.

"Is that what you want me to do? I just need you to clarify, because removing your clothes is all the end goal, but the method and intention behind it tells me how I'm going to fuck you. If you want it slow and all night long, or if you want me to ravage you."

A buzz curls around my clit at his words, and I can't wait a second longer. I'm already drenched, and a girl can only take so much.

"Just so you know, this is your fault for showing me that video," I whisper against his mouth, then I lick his lips.

Evidently that's Cassius's tipping point because suddenly he's a wild demon about to devour me, and I'm trembling with need.

He hastily yanks my top off, tossing it somewhere behind him, then he's standing, me still clinging to him. A heartbeat later I'm on my back on the couch and he's ripping my sweatpants and underwear off in a flash.

And, well, that didn't take long to end up naked. "Guess we're going for the savage method, then?" I tease him, pulling my knees together but he tsks.

He towers over me with only the faint light from outside following the contours of his muscles. The guy is huge, and what he's packing in his pants is an anaconda.

Hands on my knees, he pushes them open, and his hands travel down my thighs to where I'm burning up.

He cups my pussy, his fingers finding the blaze as he slides them between my lips. I moan, arching my back, letting my legs drop wider.

"I didn't know I needed this so much until now," I murmur.

"Eve, I knew I was going to fuck you today from the

moment I woke up this morning, along with knowing that you were going to scream for more."

I laugh at his arrogance, but when his fingers push into me, two at once, I'm zero-in on his touch. He's on his knees between my legs, saying, "Wider, and lift your hips. I want you to open for me. Now, show me everything, gorgeous."

I'm completely lost to lust because I obey him, and I'm exposed to him, giving him what he demands.

"Your pussy is a greedy little thing, sucking down on my fingers." He's ramming them into me faster, harder. My whole body's shuddering, rocking up and down, because he's not playing around.

"You're beautiful, and you've ruined me for any other girl." Then suddenly, he pushes a third finger in.

My eyes widen because nothing is small about him, and definitely not his fingers. "I don't—"

"Trust me, you can take it. Let me show you, baby. I want you dripping wet, screaming before I even stick my cock into you."

"Sweet Jesus," I cry out as he stretches me, working them slowly into me, pushing in and out, going deeper with each motion.

I'm tingling all over, the guttural sounds he makes turning me wild. "Fuck! You should see how stretched your pussy is, and my cock hurts so hard seeing you like this."

I cry out as his thumb circles around my clit, the sensation has me bucking my hips. "I can't hold on much longer. Cassius, fuck me. I want to feel you ramming into me. Give me everything."

He unleashes a growl, withdrawing his fingers. "You have no idea how much I'm craving this. I want to be your sex slave." He strips fast, and it isn't long before he stands in front of me, huge and erect. His eyes are black, and I want him even more with his demon making an appearance. Though he's never shown me the real him, other than his eyes.

"Give me love, Cassius. Give me your thick flesh. Fuck me."

He's grunting now, and kneels down on the couch between my legs. He lowers his body over me, his cock needing no guidance, as it immediately finds my entrance.

I tense in anticipation, my nipples hard, and there's no pause. Cassius unceremoniously spears into me. Ramming all the way in, stretching me with that incredible sensation that hurts and drives me insane.

I scream, my body convulsing. "Yes, I need it like that."

He's got one hand gripping the back of the couch and the other sliding under my hips, lifting me to better meet him. Then he's punching his hips forward, taking me aggressively.

I'm crying for more, feeling nothing but his cock stretching me over and over, moving savagely fast.

Growing lust floods me, my demands bouncing off the walls. "Take me like a demon."

He roars, and we're rocking the whole room now with each thrust. "Scream for me," he demands, his breathing rushed.

"Yes, more, please more." My pleas rip from my throat. "Oh, baby, just like that."

We're both bouncing and I have no idea where either of us begin or end, not that it matters when he's in fact enslaved me to his cock.

My body tightens, the sensation deepening, when the orgasm bursts over me and I'm screaming, shuddering.

"Scream it all out for me," he purrs. He's plunging into me, bellowing his own climax. He suddenly stops moving and we're locked together, both of us writhing, sweating, gasping for breath.

I'm in another galaxy, floating on euphoria, white stars dancing in my vision. Nothing in this world equals the sensation of just climaxing where I'm completely wrecked and love every second of it.

Cassius suddenly collapses on the couch alongside me, moaning. He collects me into his arms, still deeply embedded in me, his breaths heavy.

We're both still high on the most incredible rush, his breath hot in my ears. "I think I'm losing myself to you, Eve."

Is he saying what I think he's saying? I meet his gaze, both of us lost, and in that moment, the world feels like it's perfectly placed for us to be together. "Cassius I—"

"Could you two be any fucking louder? I'm pretty sure the whole block's heard you going at it," Knox interrupts us sarcastically.

We lift our heads, twisting to see him leaning a shoulder on the wall, arms dangling by his side.

"How long have you been there?" I ask with a breathy voice.

"Long enough to feel left out."

"Then you could join us," I suggest.

He smiles at me, though part of him looks a bit lost. Maybe he needs a night of sex as badly as Cassius and I.

Cassius is already chuckling. "Good, give us a few moments to clean up, Knox, then take a seat. We're about to rewatch a movie you'll enjoy."

I hide against Cassius's chest and giggle at him because if he had it his way, we'd have sex every minute of the day. But the notion of going again with Knox as well does awaken my desire.

Evidently, I'm just as horny as Cassius.

The pool deck is like this mythical oasis that only people with money can have. The men have one outfitted and tricked out with every luxury one can imagine and I'm going to take advantage. After last night's adventure with Cassius and the movie incident, not to mention Knox joining in, insisting he only wanted to watch, I didn't get a lot of sleep.

I tell myself a little break is in order. A little distraction from my reality and everything going on.

I know Dracon doesn't want me up here by myself for whatever reason, but I don't see the harm in a dip in the heated pool to soothe my muscles and ease my chaotic thoughts.

It'll be quick. He won't even know I'm gone.

Wrapped in a fuzzy robe with my bathing suit underneath, I drop a book I'd grab from the shelf in the hall on one of the lounge chairs and hurry to the edge of the water. It's freezing up here, the wind tossing up my hair and making me shiver, but once I can sink into the warm water, I'll be golden.

My plans degrade into shit pretty quickly when a hand wraps around my hair right at the back of my skull and yanks. I fly off the lounge with a screech, scrabbling to reach back and get whoever the hell holds me to let go.

"One of the perks of being able to walk in the daylight," the vampire hisses.

A scrape of teeth against the side of my neck accompanies the statement so I know I'm right that it's a bloodsucker.

Shit. Why hadn't I listened to Dracon? But I didn't think anyone would dare touch me on their property. The Tower is supposed to be safe.

"What? You can be an asshole twenty-four hours of the day rather than twelve? Good for you." I grasp his wrist, squeezing and trying to get him to release me, but he's stubborn.

The vamp drags me back into the shadows of some of the potted plants.

"You've got some balls being here at the Tower. Trying to sink your teeth into me. You know, when Dracon sees you…" I purposely trail off. Man, if only I had my high heels on now. A nice spiked stiletto through the heart sounds like a very special way to die.

"He's not going to see me." The creature snarls and tosses me to the side.

Mistake. I roll onto my side and surge to a standing position. A fist knocks into the side of my head before I have a chance to use my book to clock him good. Stars dance in front of my eyes and I stumble again, hitting the plant hard. The creature is there to grab me, and a second hit in the same sore and throbbing spot has my vision going black.

I'm not sure how long I'm out. When I finally come to, my head is pounding and the rest of me feels like recently pounded meat ready to be cooked.

I'm tied up. Again.

Sometimes it really sucks to be a human. Even a strong human with muscles for days, like I have in my legs.

Blinking to clear my eyes, the pool deck slowly swims into view. Hell, even my teeth ache; vampires might be blood-sucking jerkoffs, but they pack a punch in those undead bones.

Okay, so this isn't the same warehouse playpen I'm used to seeing when the vamps come for me. In fact, I'm right back on the lounge where I'd dropped my stuff, my robe opened to expose my bathing suit.

So cold...but with my arms tied, I can't do a damn thing about it.

The familiar tendril of fear begins just beneath my sternum, traveling up and down at the same time to land heavy in my stomach yet scald my throat.

"Ah, the princess is awake."

It's the same unfamiliar vamp who caught me and now he's looking more smug than before. But this time, he's brought a friend, one I recognize from the Lord's charity auction. What the fuck is his name? Martin? Marvin? Mar-something.

He steps forward with such an elegance, it makes

me wonder just how old he really is, even though he doesn't look older than mid-thirties. His suit is a rich coal color and lined in red thread, and he oozes wealth and power. But in a refined way, unlike Dracon.

"You want to loosen these?" I struggle against the ropes and try to sound stronger than I actually feel. "They're chafing, and I'm not feeling really kinky right now."

Much to my surprise, the Lord's leader does just that, slicing through the ropes with one of his curved claws and offering me a grin like it's a show of good faith.

I roll my wrists to get the circulation moving again. "Thanks?"

"You're welcome." His expression hardens, and five more vampires detach from the shadows behind him. "I'm sure you know why you're here, Evelyn."

"You have a death wish? Or you want a war. If it isn't either of those, please enlighten me," I answer honestly. "Marvin, right?"

"Marius. And I'm here with a proposition for you. Something that I think you'll appreciate. Finishing Franco's organization," he says, a feral glint in his eyes.

"What makes you think I'm interested in Franco? Let his scum die out on their own."

The ferocity on his face takes my breath away. "That's not an option. Join us. It's the only way we're going to take down his entire organization."

I lean forward, resisting the urge to rub that ache in my chest. "Not sure how many times I need to tell you, or maybe I just have to find a way you'll understand. I'm not going to join you, and I'm not going to help you."

I've never seen a vampire at a loss for words until now, and I can't say what I'm doing is smart. I'm probably signing my death warrant by refusing to go along with whatever they want.

But fuck this.

I'm so tired of being tossed around like a toy or a pawn for other people to use. I'm so done being a part of their game, without anyone stopping to give a rat's ass about how I feel or what I want.

Especially these stupid vampires and their feud with Franco.

I hadn't asked him to pick me up at the club and involve me in his bullshit.

"Maybe this will help change your mind about joining us." Marius snaps his fingers, and one of his little vampire underlings pulls a body from a hiding spot on the deck.

It takes a moment for me to see that it's Franco.

And that he's fucking dead.

Yelping, I scramble against the back of the lounge, like it will somehow help me disappear.

He's been dead awhile, from what I can tell. Not that I'm really familiar with corpses, but his skin has turned a mottled color, like pond scum floating on top of the water, and his eyes bulge from their sockets.

"Now you owe me a favor," Marius says softly.

"I want nothing to do with you! This isn't convincing me of anything." Well, great, now I'm screeching.

But what the hell else is a girl to do when the body of her enemy is thrown at her feet? Literally.

"We want you on our side. You're a weapon," Marius continues.

"I'm just a woman."

"No, my dear, you're not."

"What about Knox? He's a horseman! Convince him to help you."

Marius creeps closer and crouches down to bring us to eye level. "You can have whatever you want if you join us. Money, power. People who will treat you right."

I sneer at him. "You think I'm not being treated right now?"

He chuckles. "I know you're not. The Kings have made you a prisoner. They've raped you. They've belittled you."

"I can leave whenever I want," I argue automatically through a shiver. "And, trust me, every sexual encounter happened because I wanted it to."

The leaving part is not entirely true.

My gaze flicks toward Franco again, and anger slowly replaces any fear. I wanted to be the one to finish him off. Revenge. At least, the thought has repeated in my mind more often than I care to admit. Franco should have been mine to kill, and here he is. Someone got there before me.

I open my mouth to tell Marius exactly that, when a roar shakes me down to my very bones. The two of us turn in time to see a rampaging and seriously furious Dracon bursting through the door, every piece of him promising murder.

DRACON

*E*ve is gone.

I can sense it. My animal can feel her soul in danger.

The sensation of emptiness inside of me flickered at first before it grew strong enough to have me lurching from my office and following her scent.

Up to the roof, where she'd said she was going to sunbathe and read.

So how the fuck has she disappeared?

I race up to the pool deck like the hounds of hell are hot on my ass, blind to everything except an all-encompassing need to find her. To save her.

The door offers little in terms of a buffer, and instead of opening it, turning the knob, and striding forward like the in-control man I usually am, I explode through it. It takes half a second for the picture to become clear to me: Marius, a dead Franco, and Eve on the deck.

My second roar of fury ruffles Eve and does nothing to Marius. She shuffles back, eyes wide with panic.

Why the fuck is the leader of the Lords encroaching on my territory this way *again*? Is he trying to send a message, one that says he can do whatever he wants, because it sure feels that way. And there's no fucking way I'm going to allow it. My vision turns red.

Some truce.

I trudge over to them. Is Marius trying to steal Eve

away from me? He must be. Just like Dimitri had tried—they all want a piece of what's mine.

I'll rain hell on the Lords of Night. Truce be damned. He just signed his death warrant.

The vampire slowly straightens, sliding his hands into his pants pockets. Staring at me as though we're buddies and this is just a friendly hangout. I'm ready to rip his throat out.

"Marius, fuck off," I begin heatedly. "Unless you want a war on your hands."

"I just came to chat, Dracon. As friends. Oh, and offer Franco's death as a peace offering." Marius gestures toward the corpse with his nose and a slight sniff.

He's way too close to Eve for my liking, and although something in her posture relaxes at my arrival, there's still way too much fear in her eyes.

"You came to the Tower to try and steal from me?" I ask.

He's got to be out of his fucking mind. Then again, vampires. Being undead must scramble their brains, because I never took Marius for stupid, yet that's exactly what he's being now.

"We only wanted to talk," he repeats. "A friendly conversation. I simply didn't realize that Eve wanted to stay with the Kings. Otherwise, I wouldn't have asked her to join the Lords."

I draw in a deep breath, although it does nothing to calm me. "Let me see if I'm getting this straight. Okay?" I take a few steps forward, closing the distance between us, ready to explode at any moment. "You came onto *my* territory, trying to steal *my* woman out from under *my* nose, and now you're attempting to play it off as a friendly chat. You even brought this trash with you like it's some kind of parting gift?"

I barely acknowledge the stinking, rotting corpse of the mobster.

Marius nods. "Absolutely."

I don't trust a word of it. The vamp is seriously shady. I've made it my business not to trust anyone, but vampires will do anything for power. Just like me and the boys.

"I'm here as an ally. I'll even leave peacefully if that's what you want," he replies.

"Oh, I want." I flash him my teeth, silently shifting so that I stand at the edge of the lounge where Eve sits. "Now get the fuck out of here before I change my mind about letting you go peacefully."

"That's your prerogative. You can keep that." Marius gestures at Franco, before motioning for his vampires to follow him. "A show of good faith, if you will."

"I've never known you to try and prove yourself," I snap.

He shrugs, taking out his cell from his suit's breast pocket, and sends a quick text. "Perhaps there is a first time for everything."

A thunderous *thud, thud, thud* drowns out all other sounds, and wind blows violently all around us. As a massive shadow descends over the pool, I grab Eve and pull her into the protection of my arms. A helicopter hovers over the deck, close enough to make the air whip hard against us and toss over chairs and umbrellas. Eve tucks her head into my chest, and I curl around her.

As the helicopter hovers, a rope ladder is tossed down, and the Lords begin their climb. Marius is the last to go, giving me one last spearing look before making his way up the ladder and disappearing into the cockpit.

The vampires and the helicopter are gone as quickly as they arrived. Only when the noise from the propellers is gone does Eve lift her head again.

"Talk about leaving in style," she says, rubbing her lips together, unsure.

I glance over at Franco's corpse, still laying on the cement, eyes open wide like his death came as a surprise to him, too.

Wrapping her robe tighter around herself, Eve follows my gaze and shudders. "I hope Franco died painfully. I hope he got every minute of what was coming to him. I just wish I could've been the one to give it to him."

"I know." Marius's visit has me confused more than ever. Why help us by killing Franco? Just to ask for Eve's help and strengthen our truce?

I'm not so sure.

"Is Marius telling the truth?" I ask, remembering what he had said about her not wanting to leave, that she wants to be here. With us.

She blinks those wide green eyes at me. "About what, Dracon?"

"About you. Wanting to stay."

Eve sags, her shoulders rounding forward as her

chin drops to her chest. For a half a heartbeat, I clench. Tensing and wondering what she's going to say. Until finally she smiles. "Yes. I think so."

Relief is as keen as any drug, as potent as the happiest memory of my life. Her admission makes me beyond happy. And I'm not sure why.

"I'm going to fucking murder Dimitri," I growl, marching right into Dracon's trophy room, my shoulders bunched up.

This business will never surprise me. Last night, I had the best fuck of my life with Eve, and I woke up on such a high that I told myself nothing would get me down. Which was why I made my way right for Eve's room.

That was, until I got a call from one of my men on the ground, telling me we'd been attacked. Then it went downhill fast, like a damn avalanche dragging every peaceful moment I had with it.

Dracon twists around in his seat, eyebrow arching. "What happened?"

I shove my phone in his face and hit play on the video I'd been sent, showing Dimitri and his fucking gang breaking into our warehouse down by the docks where we temporarily hold our arms that have just been shipped in.

The fucker takes all of our stock, every damn last piece. Behind him, two of our guards lay on the ground, dead, shot in the head. And in the last frame, Dimitri knowingly looks up at the camera, grinning like a fuckwit, then he torches the whole warehouse.

Dracon leaps to his feet, moving across the room like a predator, snarling, "Fucking sonofabitch!"

I suck in a hard breath. "We need to go out and hunt him. This is an insult to us. Once word gets out how easily he stole from us…how long before others think we're an easy target?"

Her gives a jerk of his head. "This needs to be taken care of, but he'll go back into hiding now. Hunting him will waste time. What we need is to make him come to us." Dracon's face is red with fury, and when he gets this way, he's dangerous as fuck and capable of anything.

"Yeah, and how do we do that? I don't see that weasel agreeing to an invitation."

He raises his head, a cruel grin spreading his mouth. "He's a greedy fae prince, maybe too dangerous to confront without mass casualties. So, we lure him with what he craves most. Our merchandise."

I study Dracon, who's clenching his jaw, already pulling his phone out and sending a message to god-knows-who.

His words run over my mind, and I understand exactly what he has planned. "He'll expect us to panic and attempt to move all our stock to a safer location, which means he's watching everything we're doing."

He looks up from the screen. "Precisely. I'm counting on it. So, we set up a fake move. None of us show our faces, and leave it to our men. No one is to know but you and I that it's a setup, just in case our men are leaking information."

I nod. "Believe me, I'll make sure this looks as real as possible. We'll use the building a block down from the port. It's mostly abandoned in that industrial zone, so once we close in on them, we won't draw attention from the human police."

Dracon's hands clench into fists. "I want it done today. Set up eyes around the place, and once you see any sign of Dimitri and his men, let me know. I'll take care of this, understand?" he growls.

Silence.

I study him. I've known Dracon for a long time, and the only time he's ever asked me to back the fuck off from a job is when it's personal to him. So, is this a way of making sure he took out his revenge on the bastard for hurting Eve? Did it all come down to that?

Hurting Dimitri is up there on my list, and it irks me that Dracon wants the glory all for himself. But I'm not surprised, either.

"Just to make it clear, I want revenge, too. The asshole needs to suffer. No fast kills for him. It was fucking bad enough that the vamps stole our chance to take out Franco."

Dracon's lips curl tighter as he growls, "Then get it organized, and he will pay for what he did to Eve and for what he took from us." Dracon abruptly turns on his heel away from me, punching his desk when he reaches it. "We should have killed him that day he took Eve. Should have done this back then."

He's right, we should have. But crying about the past isn't going to solve our current problem.

I know what I need to do, and the longer I stay here, staring at his ugly mug, the more pissed I get.

Without another word, I storm out of his trophy room. I have a war to prepare for.

I shoot off several messages to my men, telling them to meet up with me in thirty minutes for an urgent meeting. Then go to the main hall, readying to get into the elevator to head off to the bar where I'm meeting my team. They rent rooms in the back for such occasions, meaning privacy and not tracking any of them to our Tower, just in case we have a rat in our group.

A flare of something red catches at the corner of my eye, distracting me. I twist around to find Eve crossing the foyer, her nose in a book so much so that she doesn't notice me. She's wearing a cute little red dress with black leggings, as well as fluffy house shoes the color of cotton candy, looking more at home with each passing day.

I study her, strolling into the main room and curling up in the corner of the couch where the sun drenches the spot through the windows. She's like a cat, drawn to heat, and not once has she lifted her head from her book. What is she reading anyway?

The temptation to join her tightens across my chest, my cock twitching just at the thought of having her soft, curvy body pressed up against me.

I can't get enough of her. She's my fucking torment, constantly in my mind, her heady scent always in my nostrils. I smell her everywhere in our Tower now. I find her long hairs on everything…even down my pants on days I haven't spent with her. Fuck if I know how that happens, but she's leaving her mark on us to ensure we don't forget she's here.

And it's driving me wild with need.

I tell myself not to get too cozy, because shit changes in our world in a heartbeat, yet the longer I have her in my life and the more times I slide my cock into her perfect little hole, the harder it gets to differentiate between enjoying her now and telling myself she may not be forever.

When the fuck did I become so pussy whipped that she consumes my every thought?

DRACON

"*D*imitri's just been spotted at the warehouse. They've fallen for the bait."

I stare at the message on my phone from Cassius, my veins on fire, fury igniting in my gut at the shit that Dimitri's been pulling. He's made a huge mistake making me his enemy.

I toss the phone on my bed and begin to rip off my clothes. I'm out on my balcony at dusk, dark enough for the humans to not make sense of what I'm about to do should any of them look up at the Tower.

I call to my dragon, my skin splitting, wings stretching outward, body shifting. I climb up and over the railing, then dive into the air.

Midway, my wings completely snap out, my body

expanding, covered in scales. I beat my wings, dragging myself higher into the darkening sky.

Rage bubbles in my chest, and I swoop through the cold air that ripples over my dragon form.

I've had enough of sitting back, of waiting. With all the shit with the horsemen, knowing that Aris will regain his memories soon, it's killing me to sit around and do nothing. Knox is constantly in a shitty mood, as he's going out on daily hunting trips for Aris and coming back empty handed. So, while that crap is going on, I don't want other assholes destroying our business.

There's no better time than now to finish this before it escalates into a full-blown war. Word will be spreading about Franco's death, too, which means gangs are already working on taking over his territory. It's something I've been working on in the background myself, getting our men to infiltrate their gang to see who the new players are. The solution is simple…eliminate anyone who thinks they stand a chance, and do a hostile takeover of his business.

My mind's been occupied of late with gaining a greater foothold in the city, especially before the Lords do. What other reason do they have for taking out Franco supposedly on our behalf? Well, aside from having an eye on Eve.

I bristle at the thought. If Marius pushes me, I'll bring a fucking war to his doorstep.

I swoop through the low-hanging clouds, the iciness chilling my body, but I unleash a roar, all my pent up anger contained in the fire blasting from my mouth.

I need to get my head straight. Never go into battle without focus.

I dive back down, the city lights sparkling brightly below, but I stay high enough to remain unseen until I reach the warehouse, keeping an eye out for Dimitri's little wyvern pet.

Skies are clear for now, and with the warehouse in sight, I scan from up here for any movement.

There's a huge truck parked out the front of the warehouse, and a stream of people are hurrying toward the warehouse from nearby cars on the quiet road. I might be too high to see faces, but I immediately spot the flickers of magic popping from Dimitri using his fae power to break into my warehouse.

Fucking predictable cunt.

I shoot back into the clouds and race dead ahead, coming down only once I'm past the warehouse.

I quickly skim low over the city, moving so fast that to most I might be mistaken as a thrashing wind.

I don't care in all honesty if anyone sees me. Only about destroying Dimitri.

Heart thundering, I lift myself on my approach with a bird's eye view of the warehouse up ahead. The rats are darting into my warehouse through the torn doors.

What they'll find are empty crates, but it's too late for them now.

A few stragglers strut inside, and that's my cue.

I propel myself through the air toward my rear of the warehouse before I pivot to my right just before reaching it. Drawing in deep breath, I can feel the fire churning in my chest. The excitement of finally making a difference.

I unleash everything I have.

A thunderous growl erupts across the night air, a blaze bursting from my gaping mouth. It glows in the night, funneling directly for the building.

Orange flames lick at the cold, hurtling for my warehouse.

I don't hold back. Fury pummels in my head, propelling the fire.

My attack strikes with such force, it buckles the metal roof. The gasoline we'd stored inside catches and it spreads instantaneously.

Fire races across the building, incinerating everything.

Fuck, it looks spectacular. My chest blooms at the great bonfire I'd created. The only thing that even compares to such beauty is my Eve.

The girl I'm completely obsessed over, and, whether she knows it or not, there is no future where she doesn't end up mine.

I'll destroy the whole fucking city or anyone who stands in my way. Anyone who hurts her won't see me coming.

It's been too long since I've played the nice guy. And you sure as fuck don't win a war or spark terror in your enemies by following the rules.

I catapult myself up and over the burning building, the flames tickling my underbelly. At the entrance, a couple of men are shouting, attempting to escape.

I see nothing but red fury.

No one is getting out.

Fire spews past my mouth, burning them to a crisp in seconds. That's all it takes with dragon fire.

Adrenaline spikes through my veins, and I'm reveling in the sounds of screams piercing the night.

Not a shred of guilt chews me up. Not a fucking inch when I picture the state we found Eve in after Dimitri got his hands on her. After seeing the video of him stealing from me.

When you find rats in your home, you stamp them out or they'll take over.

Batting my wings, I hover over the roaring blaze, staring down at my handy work, rather pleased, more so to not see anyone else escaping. The black SUVs parked on the curb are on fire too, adding to the light show.

Sirens ring in the distance.

I roar, that taste of frustration in my throat that they'll put out my creation.

The electric taste of magic on my tongue is nonexistent.

Each asshole who entered my warehouse has perished, and before I go anywhere, I need to make sure Dimitri is gone. I won't walk away without knowing.

An explosive screech taints the air, and my chest hardens. I jerk my attention up to Dimitri's pet.

The wyvern is diving, coming right for me, its spiked tail whipping from side to side in preparation for its attack.

My pulse speeds up.

I've done my research on these fucking critters.

Don't let it strike me with its tail or I'll be knocked out for days again. The rest of him is fair game.

With a cruel snarl, I turn and throw myself up at him, a growl exploding from my mouth. My flames do nothing to him, but my eyes are locked on his barbed tail.

His tail is poised for attack.

We're close…too close.

The tail sweeps around his body, coming right for me.

Heart in my throat, I hurl myself left at the last second, the tail missing me by inches. But in the same move, I slash out a clawed paw, striking the beast right under its chin. Turns out it's a wyvern's weak point.

Black blood spurts out, and he screeches, the sound ear-piercing.

That's my chance, and I take it. I pivot in midair and swing back around. Mouth gaping open, I charge down toward the beast and savagely bite down on the thick part of its tail that holds no poisonous thorns. With a vicious shake of my head, I sink my teeth in and tear it right off him.

Blood floods my mouth and I spit the tail out, the pungent taste making me gag.

The animal swings around toward me, bleeding, howling in pain. But the fucker isn't going down.

It hurls itself at me, and I don't hold back. Except, it can't hurt me.

We clash, and it's a battle to the end.

Claws and teeth, we tear into each other, the asshole rips into my shoulder.

Anger bleeds through me, the pain barely noticeable, but this time when I slam into him, my head cracks into his. The distinct crack of breaking bone resonates and I know I've done my part.

With a final whine and exhale of breath, the creature's wings flop by his side, and he drops out of the sky.

By the time the creature hits the concrete road with a splat, he's in his human form, naked and covered in a growing pool of his own blood.

A snarl in my throat, I turn myself away from the dead dragon and come in for a sharp landing. Already I'm pulling back my dragon and by the time I land, it's my human feet touching the cold sidewalk. My back knits up with my wings tucked away.

Sirens blare, sounding closer, so I don't have much time.

I sprint toward the burning building...well, what's left of it. Smoke billows into the night sky, curling like shadows.

The smoke and flames have no impact on a dragon like me. Half the roof has collapsed, the rest holding, but it won't be long.

I scan the charred dead, hurrying over the debris, counting at least a dozen bodies. It doesn't take me long to notice a faint blue haze glowing farther to my left where part of the roof remains intact.

Fae magic.

I sprint over there and shove aside a fallen shelf. Underneath, lies Dimitri, a gaping hole in the side of his head, blood pouring out. The rest of him is burnt, and his death brings me a sense of calm.

Hovering over him is the blue light haze that slowly ascends. It's said that fae can never be truly killed, and once they lose their mortal body, they transcend to their next realm of existence.

As long as it's not anywhere near fucking Earth, then I bid him farewell.

Just as I am leaving the building, cop cars come racing down the road, followed by fire engines. Their lights pulsing amid the smoke and night.

Not wanting to get caught explaining any of this, I quickly duck around the side of the building and race toward the backyard, my dragon already tearing out of me.

I'm soaring through the night sky in no time, and when I glance back down, a sense of completion floods me.

I came to do what we should have done long ago. I refuse to call it revenge, and see it more as paying back a favor.

Swinging to the right, I sweep toward home, leaving behind the monsters who dared touch something that belonged to me.

When I reach the Tower, I land on the roof, shedding my dragon form. The cold wind bits into my skin, and what I long for now is a hot shower and a glass of whiskey.

One of my enemies has been eradicated and it's time to have one drink to send them off, and for me to celebrate.

Using the elevator, I'm down in the main area in moments, but the moment I step out of the lift, I'm greeted by Cassius, Knox, and Eve.

They're all holding onto pizza boxes, the savory smell coaxing my gut into a growl. "Good timing. I'm hungry."

They blink at me, well mostly Eve, since coming home naked and bleeding is normal for us. Knox shrugs at my presence and strolls into the main room.

"What the hell happened to you?" Eve's eyes are wide, and I love seeing her so concerned. "You're bleeding and, oh my god, are you burned?"

I glance down and brush ash from my hip. It falls like black snow to the floor. "A dragon can't burn, gorgeous."

"What you are is a smelly mess. You reek of fire," Cassius adds, his stare growing intense. "Been having fun out there?" He arches an eyebrow, because he knows exactly where I've been, and I sense his jealousy. But this was a job I needed to complete alone.

"I'm fine." I meet Eve's worried stare instead. "In fact, I'm more than fine. And I'm starving."

"Okay," she says in slow motion. "Maybe clean up and then you can join us. Then you can tell us where you've been."

Cassius is eyeing me, his stare narrowing. "Do I want to know?"

"Dimitri will no longer be a problem. That's all you need to know. He will never pose a danger to any of us. He's paid with his life for what he's done to you, Eve."

She's blinking faster now, and for a moment, I'm

convinced I see tears in her eyes. She pushes a cute grin on her sweet lips. "Well then, hurry and wash up. We need to celebrate."

Those words shouldn't impact me as much as they do, but to give her security brings me a rush of adrenaline. If it takes destroying every one of our enemies to protect her, then I'm up for the challenge.

Fuck the harmony of our packs. I'm ready for change.

CHAPTER NINETEEN

KNOX

The charred husk of the warehouse greets us down at the dock. Those goddamn Russians had it coming. Taking our stock, killing our men, trying to move into our city—I don't blame Dracon for burning them all.

But with so many of our men dead and our weapons destroyed from the blaze, what's left to be salvaged?

Today we need to make sure there are no surprises. No one can get the better of us.

"Stop looking like you expect the sky to fall," Dracon growls at me.

I shrug, unconcerned, casting him a cruel smile of my own. "Won't it, though?"

"He's right. We do seem to have some shitty luck," Cassius adds, while keeping Eve close to his side.

The stench of embers and ash burn the inside of my nostrils, and I swallow down a wave of revulsion and rage.

"Keep an eye out for anything we can save," Dracon

says unnecessarily, striding a step ahead of us, his gaze sweeping the wreckage.

I growl under my breath.

In the back of my mind, I'm thinking about Aris. I don't understand why no one else is taking his presence on this plane as seriously as I am. Russians and gang feuds seem a lot less important when stacked next to a horseman of the apocalypse, in my opinion, but what the fuck do I know?

This fucking hunt for Aris… It feels never ending. It feels like I'll spend the rest of my eternal life hunting that son of a bitch down only to have him one step ahead of me, even without his memories.

My feet crunch over debris as I stalk into the ruined cavern of the warehouse like some great dead beast's belly.

"Look at this shit," Dracon mutters under his breath.

That's all I see—shit. Dimitri and his goons left nothing for us to salvage. His plan, of course, because only a fool would leave a scrap.

Cassius groans and helps Eve over a pile of scrap wood that I swear is still smoking.

"If I could kill them all over again, I'd do it with pleasure." Dracon grits through his teeth.

"And leave nothing for the rest of us, of course," Cassius adds with obvious snark.

The fine hairs on the back of my neck stand at attention and I jerk around, staring into the gloom of the water and seeing nothing.

"I'm so sorry," Eve murmurs. "For everything."

"Not like it's your fault," Cassius replies.

Dracon whirls around with a glare for everyone. "Is it not?"

"Don't talk to her with that fucking tone, dude." Cassius sounds pissed.

But there's something here. Something seething beneath the surface and begging for my attention. I can't look at him. I can't look at Eve.

A crack rips through the otherwise clear sky, and now my skin breaks out in goosebumps.

"Fuck!" I have just enough time to roar out the curse before Aris rips a hole open in the space in front of us.

His red charger snorts smoke from its widened nostrils and Aris grips the reins tightly. There's madness and chaos about him. His eyes aren't quite focused the way I remember them. His memories aren't fully back yet—Cassius's spell still has some hold over him. Lucky for us.

Without his helmet, he looks lost, until he fixes his gaze on me. His dark hair is wild around his face, his facial hair no longer neatly trimmed, and his fiery pupils burning like hot coals inside his skull.

"You!" he shouts out.

I slowly straighten.

Talk of the fucking devil, or whatever it is Cassius always says.

His crimson armor looks dented and stained. Dirtied in a way I know he'd never tolerate or allow if he had his full memories at his disposal.

Dismounting, he slams a palm against his horse's rump. The poor thing charges forward with a nicker and bolts off, disappearing into the fog rolling in over the water.

"Seriously?" Cassius asks with a dry, incredulous laugh. "Now?"

Ignoring him, I focus entirely on Aris.

"What did you do to me?" Aris growls. He takes a single step in our direction, followed by another. Then he squeezes his eyes shut and shakes his head, as if something pains him.

When he opens his eyes again, they're blazing with fury. "I'm going to gut you. I'll gut you and leave you groveling in front of me."

A snarl burns my throat in retaliation. "Only one of us will bleed before the end of this." I sweep a hand out to the others in a silent bid for them to stay back.

I don't need to look at them to know the expression Dracon wears, hearing him scoff. Yet rage swims in my blood as Aris's bewildered expression shifts into a cocky fucking smirk when he sees Eve.

"My, my. You just bring her out with you?" he asks. "You allow her loose?"

I don't even want him to *look* at my little dove. It awakens the old me, the creature I used to be before my scythe broke. Before this man's madness took everything.

"Shut the fuck up," I snap at him.

Then, before he has a chance to set his sights fully on Eve, I charge him.

Aris snarls right as I reach out to slam my fist against his cheek. The force of the hit fueled by hatred knocks him back a step before he understands what I've done.

Death flashes in his eyes before he hits me back. His fist is a damn rock sending spasms of pain along my torso as he lands it right in my kidney.

"Do your worst, you fucking asshole." I tilt my head back and spit into his face.

The moment of pain is forgotten as he charges me, the cage of his arms keeping me from hitting him again.

He sends us sprawling, me landing hard on my back, knocking the air from my lungs. His hand firmly clutches one arm as the other rises to my neck.

Darkness filters my vision for a brief moment when he squeezes.

"I might not know you, but I know you're a stain on my life," he growls out, jaw clenched, teeth bared. "I know your death will free me."

"But you can't kill me," I sputter through my closing throat. "Not without the blade."

"Knox!" Eve's terrified voice rings out like an alarm. Aris's gaze shifts to her, and it's the split second I need to throw myself against Aris. He rolls with me on top of him, and I bring my knee up between his legs.

He swings his body at the last minute so that my hit lands on his hip rather than where I intend. I throw a punch into his jaw instead, but even though black blood splatters across the dock, he only laughs and laughs.

I need to end him, once and for all. And that means I need the Mortem Blade.

As I reach for its handle on my belt, Aris somehow untangles himself from my hold, pushes himself to stand, and launches himself at my little dove. Cassius and Dracon move in front of her, creating a wall, while I scramble to follow after him, leaping on his back and throwing wild punches at the side of his head. He catches my arm and slams me down to the ground again while I thrash.

"No, don't! Stop it! Stop it!" Eve's yelling again, but not at me. Not at Aris. At herself.

I squeeze my eyes shut as she screams, and a blast of power rolls out over the area. The earth shakes beneath us, the wood of the dock splintering in some places. Waves ripple over the dark water in the harbor, powerful enough to make the boats rock and crash into each other.

I feel the echo of her power more than the earth. As a horseman, our powers are stronger when we're together. We are known to amplify each other's gifts, and it seems even Eve is affected by it.

She may not have meant to unleash the magical boom, but my stomach clenches and my eyes blur from it just the same. Every bone in my body aches.

"Shit," I groan. She's fucking strong.

When I look at Aris, I see his muscles are tense, his body cracking and jerking against mine. In the span of a few seconds he seems to grow heavier until he sighs. Relieved.

Recognition flashes over his face, and dread seizes me.

"Ah." It's a low, drawn-out sound. "That's much better." His smile flashes hotter and brighter. "Wouldn't you agree, Knox? About fucking time."

Ah, shit.

The terrifying pulse of my heart makes my head swim even as reality bites deep.

He's got his fucking memories back. Somehow, whatever Eve did, the blast of magic she sent his way, brought his memories surging home again. The spell has lost its hold over him.

Now we're all going to die.

Fuck.

EVE

I've seriously fucked up. More than I have in my life until this point. My gut reaction to help Knox got us right out of the frying pan and into the inferno of Hell. The power ripped out of me without thinking. Wanting to save Knox. Being so damn terrified of Aris showing up here, now, feeling so unprepared—

And look what I've done.

I see it the moment Aris lifts his head to me and smiles. Like he's just won a ten-million-dollar lottery jackpot and he's somehow escaped paying taxes on it.

Suddenly he's staring at me from a foot away, blood dripping down the side of his check but he's not cut. Knox's blood.

"No." I somehow manage to speak before pawing at Cassius. At Dracon. At anyone who might be able to keep this being from getting his hands on me.

Terror turns every nerve in my body to acid.

The men waste no time jumping into the fight. Dracon leaps forward with a snake hiss, landing a powerful blow to the side of Aris's head. Aris's eyes flicker over me a final time, pressing down on me hard enough I want to cry out, before he sends a blaze of fire to pry Dracon away from him.

I grit my teeth and another blast of my power shoots out toward Aris. He slides back on the dock, the blast pushes him face a few feet, but not strong enough to send him flying.

He looks impressed. "Once you learn how to harness that power inside you, Daughter of Chaos, you and I will rule the cosmos."

Goosebumps run up and down my arms, like they always do whenever he calls me his daughter.

Knox shifts into shadows behind him, disappearing from sight, while Cassius moves to stand at my side, and I curse this entire situation. The panic inside of me demands I do something to alleviate it, knowing nothing will change anytime soon.

A tremendous growl tears from Dracon's lips as he changes forms. A flash of triumph lights his face as his human figure tears away to reveal an enormous dragon.

"Aw, cute," Aris says with a grin. "Now watch this."

Unfazed, he reaches out and grabs my arm. I yell as he hauls me to his side. With the other arm, he reaches out and the growing ball of flames in the back of Dracon's throat freezes. Somehow, he's able to stop Dracon's fire blast from fully unleashing. The dragon chokes.

Knox and his shadows attack from behind us, sliding

along my skin and coating me with darkness as they reach for Aris. Those shadows wrap around his wrists and break his restraining hold on me. I grunt and fall to the floor while the shadows dive and dip, chasing Aris, though he maintains his hold on Dracon.

Aris clicks his tongue. "So silly, you four are. It's really a fantastic display of mortal idiocy at its finest. Fire doesn't affect me, Apex. I *manipulate* fire."

"How about guns, then, asshole?" Cassius comes out of nowhere with a massive rifle raised and pointed at the horseman's head.

Fuck yes!

With Knox's shadows holding him down, Aris can't move as Cassius pulls the trigger.

Bang, bang, bang!

Sparks light up the darkness and gunfire explodes against the silence of the sleeping city. Aris grunts, his body shaking as the bullets pelt him in rapid fire, but they begin to shoot back out of him in different directions. It's like he's made of fucking rubber or something. The bullets whizz dangerously close to us all, and Cassius and I dive onto our stomachs to avoid being hit. Dracon takes to the skies.

Knox has his blade out and swipes at his turned back, but Aris senses it and sidesteps. The edge embeds into the dock's wooden planks.

Aris kicks Knox in the stomach, spins, and then roundhouse kicks him again in the head. Knox stumbles, his hand leaving the Mortem Blade's handle momentarily, but Aris sees his opening and goes for it.

I have to do something. That blade is the only thing

that can kill a horseman. With it, Aris can destroy worlds. Universes.

Gathering strength in my low belly, trying to concentrate on Aris—and Aris alone—my entire body tingles, and I let a wave of magic tear from me again.

The explosion funnels outward, the blast ten times more powerful in this concentrated state. Aris must realize that too because he leaps out of the way just as it lands where he stood a second ago. The Mortem Blade is ripped out of the ground and spins across the dock, toward the edge of the water.

"No!" Knox is off and running for it. As the blade disappears over the edge, so does Knox, and their dual splashes follow soon after.

Aris rises, holding his jaw and resetting it into place. He winces, but besides that, he shows no other sign of pain or injury.

"It's so strange. You're mine, and yet you're so average. Inadequate. How long do you think you and your silly little friends will be able to keep this up?"

"I can do this all fucking day," Cassius shouts from behind me. "Eve, down!"

I barely have time to drop before he unloads another flurry of bullets right into Aris's face.

I feel the bite of the bullet when it buries into my upper arm, and I cry out, grasping it. It takes me too long to realize I've been hit with one of the rogue bullets that have bounced off Aris. Fire trails down from my bicep all the way down to my finger, and draws a shudder of pain that has me curling into a ball. My palm comes back painted red with blood.

"Eve!"

I'm not sure which of the Kings yell my name. It sounds like Knox. It might be Cassius. Or Dracon, but my eyes blur and I struggle to contain my fear as pain radiates from the wound, blood dripping down onto the ground.

When I look up, I find armor-plated boots in front of me. Fear speeds my pulse as I scramble to my knees, still gripping my wound. I try to reach for my chaotic magic again, but with so much pain biting into my arm, I can't concentrate long enough to grab hold of it.

"Pathetic. All mortals are *pathetic.*" Aris spits the last word as he peers down at me from his hooked nose.

His hand outstretches, reaching for me, but then his eyes flick to the right and he freezes in place, fingers inches from my neck.

When I follow his gaze, I see the sharp curved edge of the Mortem Blade hovering dangerously close to his neck. The blue light the ancient relic emits sizzles over it, and I can feel the icy prick of the horrible death it promises.

In the next second, Knox solidifies behind Aris, his chest heaving and water dripping from his clothes and black hair.

"Touch her and die," he threatens.

Aris lifts his hand away from me without hesitation.

I don't move. Don't breathe.

"I've been waiting so long to cleave your head from your shoulders," Knox whispers, that raw hunger for death I'd seen back in the shed with the Russian flaring in his eyes again.

"Looks like you're going to have to have to wait a little longer, brother," Aris replies, and a grin lifts his lips.

His chin lifts, and a massive shadow stretches over us.

Everything happens so fast, I struggle to comprehend it. Aris throws himself to the left, away from the blade, and Knox leaps back just as a colossal wolf bounds over me and lands on top of Knox. The Mortem Blade drops from his hand, landing feet away, and when the wolf's form starts to recede, I realize it's Dracon who tried to sneak attack Aris. Instead, his claws puncture Knox's chest.

"Get the fuck off me!" Knox bellows as Dracon shifts back into his human form. "You fucking idiot!"

Cassius's and my gaze lock from across the dock, and when we both spot Aris running for the Mortem Blade, Cassius takes off to get there first.

He's not fast enough.

When Aris lifts the death blade into the air in triumph, Cassius skids to a halt. Fear widens his eyes.

Then, a blaze of fire erupts around Aris, as if Hell's opened up right there at the harbor, and the flames twist around him into a tornado. I'm smacked in the face with the searing heat of it, and it momentarily steals the breath from my lungs.

When the fire extinguishes, the horseman is gone.

And so is the Mortem Blade.

"Shit!" Knox yells, shoving Dracon off him and jumping to his feet. After walking across the scorched dock where Aris just stood, he turns to the sky and unleashes a roar loud enough to fill the heavens.

"What the fuck just happened?" Cassius demands, punching the side of his own head in frustration. "We had him!"

Dracon pushes himself up, his entire body trembling with defeat.

"Goddamn it, Drac! What was that? Knox had him!" Cassius says.

"I know, I know!" Dracon says. His voice is raspy, probably from Aris's hold on his fire as a dragon. But there's pain in there too. Not physical pain. Something deeper. "I fucked up. I fucked up again."

Throwing his hands in the air, Cassius scoffs. "Your ego couldn't handle Aris manhandling you for even a second, could it?"

Dracon doesn't even respond.

"Shut it, Cassius," I snap. "You're not helping any."

"We're fucked! We're fucked!" he repeats as he paces back and forth. Knox hasn't breathed another sound, his back turned away from us, and I don't know what's more disturbing—his furious silence, or when he's loud and unchained.

Above us, lightning flashes behind the clouds, zigzagging across the sky. The little hairs on my arms rise as the energy around us increases tenfold, and for a second, I wonder if it's Aris coming back to finish us all off with Knox's blade.

Feeling the tension build, Knox slowly turns. More lightning cracks across the darkness, and then the sky splits, a seam opening with a second resounding boom.

My blood curdles as two huge horses descend from a stream of billowing fog.

Not Aris. Much worse.

For the first time, I see genuine fear on Knox's face, and that makes acid spin in my gut.

"What the fuck—" Cassius gasps as the two riders come more into view. Their steeds land on the dock, the wood groaning under their tremendous weight.

"Knox." The woman rider grips her reins tightly, her skin the color of night and her horse the palest cream I've ever seen. High cheekbones and regal features make her as beautiful as she is terrifying. Her long white braids are twisted into a knot on the top of her head that reminds me of a bale of hay. "It's been a long time."

Knox straightens with his shoulders thrown back and a petulant expression darkening his handsome features.

"Opia," he says through clenched teeth. Then he glances at her riding partner, a man with a shrunken face and cloudy eyes. "Brone. Of course you both show up now. Especially since I've been stuck on this plane for centuries."

These must be the missing two horsemen. Famine and Pestilence.

Oh fuck…

Dracon comes to my side and helps me stand, his gaze steely and his lips a thin line. Cassius touches my uninjured shoulder to tell me he's close, too.

Brone's whited-out eyes pierce through me in a gaze that sees everything. Probably even the color of my panties. And I shiver.

"You understand the nature of our visit," he says in a slithering tone.

Knox growls, "I have a few ideas."

"The woman." Opia uses her nose to gesture to me. "She's powerful."

"She's half-mortal," Knox replies.

I want to shrink into a little ball and curl away until they all disappear. Is that a possibility?

"The woman needs to die." Brone's voice is dry, barely a whisper, but those simple words spear through me. "She cannot be allowed to live."

"You should be punishing Aris for this," Knox says. "He's gone against our rules. He impregnated a mortal."

"Aris will be dealt with," Opia snaps. "But five horsemen? This cannot be. There is an imbalance of power. Everything will crumble into oblivion."

"She's not powerful enough to be one of you," Dracon shouts to the ethereal being, snapping her attention his way.

Her lip curls up in disgust. "You dare speak to me about matters you know nothing of, Apex?"

"I do," he answers without a hint of fear in his voice. "Eve belongs to the Kings of Eden. She's ours."

Brone snorts a laugh. "What a fool."

Opia shakes her head, not wanting to be bothered by Dracon, and turns her attention back to Knox. "If you think what the Apex says is true, Knox, then I'm here to inform you that you're very, *very* wrong."

"Kn-Knox?" I stammer, my heart pounding inside my chest. I'm waiting for him to say something, to defend me, to plead my case to these otherworldly beings.

But he doesn't do any of those things. He glances at me over his shoulder, his expression unreadable, and my anxiety begins to climb.

He wouldn't just give me up to Opia and Brone. Right?

No, he wouldn't.

Would he?

"Move. The girl is stronger than you can even imagine." Opia draws her own long skinny blade from the holster at her hip and points it my way. "She will be the end of all of us. The end of everything as we know it. She must die."

Then, to my absolute horror, Knox steps aside.

"I'm sorry, little dove."

ABOUT MILA YOUNG

Best-selling author, Mila Young tackles everything with the zeal and bravado of the fairytale heroes she grew up reading about. She slays monsters, real and imaginary, like there's no tomorrow. By day she rocks a keyboard as a marketing extraordinaire. At night she battles with her mighty pen-sword, creating fairytale retellings, and sexy ever after tales. In her spare time, she loves pretending she's a mighty warrior, walks on the beach with her dogs, cuddling up with her cats, and devouring every fantasy tale she can get her pinkies on.

Ready to read more and more from Mila Young?www.subscribepage.com/milayoung

www.milayoungbooks.com
For more information...
milayoungauthor@gmail.com

ABOUT HARPER A. BROOKS

Harper A. Brooks lives in a small town on the New Jersey shore. Even though classic authors have always filled her bookshelves, she finds her writing muse drawn to the dark, magical, and romantic. But when she isn't creating entire worlds with sexy shifters or legendary love stories, you can find her either with a good cup of coffee in hand or at home snuggling with her furry, four-legged son, Sammy.

RONE AWARD WINNER
USA TODAY BESTSELLING AUTHOR
INTERNATIONAL BESTSELLING AUTHOR

Want to read more from Harper A. Brooks? Subscribe to Harper's newsletter and get *Halfling for Hire* for free! http://BookHip.com/MCBDCN

www.ingramcontent.com/pod-product-compliance
Lightning Source LLC
Chambersburg PA
CBHW020745190726
48285CB00006B/1882